THE HOUSE OF TWELVE

By Sean Davies

Contents

PROLOGUE

Strange images of her family flashed through her mind amongst violent red flashes, and were interrupted only by eerie still pictures of household interiors. Bricked up windows, sealed doors and overwhelming visions of endless darkness flowed into her turbulent dream. Along with them came pleasant yet creepy music, like the type that played in elevators and telephone on-hold tracks, and it droned through her skull relentlessly. As irritating as it was, for some strange reason she feared more than anything that it would end.

DAY 1

Sarah awoke from her nightmare and stretched her arms out wide before opening her eyes. Her vision was hazy, and after struggling to focus her eyes on the ceiling she suddenly realised that she was very cold and uncomfortable. With a great deal of effort, she moved herself upright and almost fell off the brown sofa that she had been laying on. Staring at a large old-fashioned television set that was before her, along with a glass coffee table and black leather-bound menu that was lying atop it, Sarah rubbed her eyes and blinked until they came into proper focus. As she looked around the living room and listened to the eerie music that was playing constantly in the background, a shiver far more powerful than that of her mere physical chill ran down her spine. It wasn't her house.

The foreign room in which she found herself had faded terracotta and cream patterned wallpaper that was beginning to peel away at the edges, and a dark red carpet. It was a long living room and dining room that, judging by the ceiling, had been knocked into one somewhere in the house's history. Beside her there were three brown armchairs that matched the sofa, and a black iron fireplace with a strange looking clock sitting atop the mantelpiece. There were two wooden doors at either end of the room, and a big polished wood dining table with eight matching vintage chairs at the opposite end of the room to Sarah. Most disturbing of all were the three bricked-up windows, one on the short wall beside where she was sitting and two on the wall opposite the doors. Looking away from the brickwork, she realised with a gasp that she was not alone. There were other people in the room, people she did not know.

There were two people slumped over on the dining table; an attractive young Asian woman and a chubby man in his early forties, their faces resting uncomfortably on the hard wood. Beside Sarah on one of the armchairs was a handsome auburn-haired man in his late twenties or early thirties with a fashionably trimmed beard. She tried to force herself to edge away quietly, but her body was responding as sluggishly as her mind.

The auburn-haired man stirred and looked around wildly, before his gaze finally rested on her. He stared into her blue eyes with his own fearful green ones.

"Why am I here?" he stammered.

"I was going to ask you the same thing," Sarah replied cautiously.

"I don't know. I can't remember much. What's your name?" he asked with equal caution.

"Sarah... Fischer, I think." Even that knowledge seemed slightly distant to her.

"I'm Lucas Adams." He pressed his fingers to his temples and clenched his eyes shut. "Apart from that, nothing." He opened his eyes and dropped his hands onto his lap. "I can remember my Dad and my house... the rest is just red. Red and painful."

"I remember my sister and her daughters... a bit," Sarah slurred. "Oh, and her husband." Something else almost came into her mind, before disappearing under a pulse of pain that surged through her head.

"I wonder where we are," Lucas said, looking at the nearest bricked up window.

"Maybe they know?" Sarah said, pointing towards the people at the dining table.

Lucas forced himself up out of the armchair and staggered towards the fireplace. He picked up an iron poker, and after a moment of brief hesitation he picked up another for Sarah. She lifted her tired body off the sofa and slowly accepted the improvised melee weapon from Lucas, and together they advanced towards the other end of the room.

The Asian girl and the chubby man groaned and lifted their heads from the table before Lucas and Sarah could get anywhere close to them. They looked at each other in confusion, and then turned their attention towards the poker-wielding individuals standing in the middle of the room.

"I haven't done anything wrong!" the chubby man with short curly black hair said frantically. "Please don't hurt me!"

"What do you want?" the Asian girl asked aggressively.

Lucas lowered his poker and gestured for Sarah to do the same. "Nothing. We don't know why we're here, to be honest, and we were hoping that you did," he said diplomatically. "Do you know where we are, or remember anything?"

"I'm Komo," the long-haired Asian girl said confidently, until she struggled to recall her last name. "Komo... Hattori..."

"I'm Carl Smith, I think," the chubby man said with a fearful voice.

"Do you remember how we got here?" Sarah pressed.

"All I remember is a car waiting for me, and some money," Komo said. "Everything else just hurts my head."

Carl shook his head. "I can't remember anything, just my name. Sorry."

"Does anyone else hear that music?" Komo asked, looking around to see where it originated from.

"Faintly," Sarah said. "Maybe it's coming from upstairs."

"We should take a look around," Lucas said bravely.

"I'll stay here," Carl said nervously. "I don't feel that well..."

"Then let's hope that whoever brought us here doesn't turn up while we're gone," Komo said unkindly.

Carl shivered but stayed sitting where he was.

The door near the sofa and television opened, and once again Sarah and Lucas brandished their sharp pokers. A big brutish man with harsh facial features and the build of a lumberjack walked casually into the room. There was a long knife in his hand.

"Any of you know why we're in this fucking house?!" he barked angrily.

The group stayed where they were and shook their heads slowly.

"Just fucking great," the big brute said to himself. "We've got four more in here," he called into the hallway.

"There's more?" Sarah asked.

"Yeah, blondie," he answered. "We're up to twelve so far."

"If you can count the snivelling wreck in the hallway," a gorgeous redheaded woman said, barging into the room. "Oh my, I can see we've got at least one more real man in the building." She flicked her long red curls and smiled at Lucas.

"You're making me jealous," a confident male voice said from behind the large man.

"You two should take this more seriously," the brute chided.

"I'm telling you, this is just some crazy prank," the redhead said cheerfully. "My girlfriends pull this kind of stuff all the time."

"What if it isn't?" he growled back.

"What if we've been kidnapped by some psycho?" Carl whimpered.

"It's quite likely," Lucas said gravely, "but it's a bit strange how they've just left us free to roam around."

"They could've changed their minds," Komo said thoughtfully. "Chickened-out or something half way through whatever they were planning."

"Oh god, I hope so, I hope we can get out!" Carl said, putting his hands over his face in distress.

"Listen to you lot," Jessica said in a snide tone. "I'm telling you, this is just a joke or something. We could be on a reality TV show!" she added excitedly, looking around for cameras.

"You're fucking nuts," the brutish man sighed.

"Maybe introductions are in order?" Sarah suggested.

"Definitely," the redhead said as she approached Lucas. "I'm Jessica Pratt, no memory, et cetera," she said, taking Lucas' hand and shaking it softly. "The big guy is Mitch–"

"Mitchell Owens," the large man cut in, and moved himself out of the way of the door.

Sarah looked critically at Jessica, who was still holding onto Lucas' hand and gazing at him with puppy dog eyes. "I'm Sarah. That's Komo and Carl. The person you're clinging to is Lucas," she said dryly.

Jessica looked amused by the disapproval in the blonde's blue eyes and let go of Lucas' hand. "I can see someone's already got dibs on you."

"Good thing, too," said a confident and very handsome man in a grey suit as he made his way slowly into the room, the same person who had spoken earlier from behind Mitchell. "No offense, Lucas, but I don't like competition. I'm Jack Thomson."

Lucas went red but spoke firmly. "I think Mitchell is right – we could be in serious trouble here."

Jack and Jessica sighed and shrugged before sitting down at the dining table, away from the almost unnoticeable Carl.

"Everyone get in here!" Mitchell shouted. He slotted the knife into his belt and sat at one end of the table.

It wasn't long before they were joined by the other confused and hesitant residents. There was Melanie Lane, a tired looking woman with black and grey hair, who could only remember that her daughters would be waiting for her; 'Lucky' Leo Davis, a slightly overweight but still attractive black-haired man in a black pinstriped suit, who only remembered a love for gambling; Jacob Anderson, a tall, plain looking boy who only remembered that he had a university lecture that he was meant to be attending; Dan Turner, a grey-haired man who claimed to be in his late forties but could have easily passed for sixty, and only remembered that he had a wife but currently cared more about finding a stiff drink; and finally, there was 'the Wreck', a craven middle-aged man who Mitchell had to coax out of the hallway. All they could get out of him was how dead they all were. It didn't do much to lift the spirits of the residents.

"The door is thick metal and won't budge an inch," Lucky said with concern, as they were discussing what they had seen of the house so far.

"I could try picking the lock," Komo said from afar. Her attention span was limited so she had taken to searching around the room whilst the group talked.

"No lock, I'm afraid," Lucky replied sadly. "Just a pretty stiff letter box."

"We should have a proper look around," Sarah suggested. "There might be a way out, or at least some brickwork that isn't as sturdy as the rest."

"If you can find me a hammer I can start making my way through it," Mitchell added helpfully.

"We'll have to keep an eye out for food if there's no easy way out," Lucas said grimly. "We could be here a while."

"Jack and I will look out for cameras," Jessica said, taking the handsome man's arm. "You'll all be praising me when I prove we're on television."

"Okay," Sarah said dryly. "I suppose it is a possibility."

Komo's concentration was fixed on the strange old clock on the mantelpiece. "Guys, have you seen this?"

"What? A clock isn't really worth our time at the minute," Melanie chided harshly.

"Fine, whatever," Komo said, making her way to the old television set. She flicked through channel after channel of grey static while the rest of the residents discussed worst-case scenarios, before giving up and moving to the coffee table.

"Twenty-three, twenty-four, twenty-three, twenty-four," the Wreck sobbed to himself.

"So it's agreed," Sarah finalised above the poor man's mad dismay. "We'll split up and look around."

"Hopefully we'll find an easy way out," Lucas replied.

"Something alcoholic would be nice, too," Dan grumbled.

"Guys, seriously, you need to see this!" Komo shouted. She had picked up the strange menu that was on the glass coffee table, and her eyes flicked between it and the clock.

"The grownups are busy," Melanie said harshly.

"The grownups need to fucking listen!" Komo hissed back.

"What is it?" Sarah asked, disturbed by the girl's tone.

"Rules," Komo said fearfully.

"House rules, house rules!" the Wreck shrieked.

Most of the group walked towards her, noting the strange clock that she had tried to point out to them earlier. It had a white circular face and only one metal hour hand behind its glass cover, but instead of being numbered up to twelve it went all the way up to twenty-four like a digital clock, and the space between twenty-three and twenty-four was coloured blood red. The hand was currently halfway in-between twelve and one; if it was accurate, then they had awoken in the strange house around midday.

Sarah took the leather-bound 'rules' from the shaken Komo to see for herself. 'The House Rules' was imprinted in large gold letters on the side that had been face down on the table when she'd awoken, and she opened it to find a list of writing laminated within its bindings.

"Welcome to The House of Twelve," Sarah read aloud. "Please find below the simple rules regarding your incarceration here. Your situation may seem bleak and hopeless, but just remember: *redemption is the key to escape.*"

"See? Reality TV," Jessica boasted proudly.

"Let her finish," Mitchell growled.

"Yes, shut up, you silly little air-head," Melanie snapped.

"Fuck you, grandma," Jessica hissed.

"Whoa, calm down!" Lucas yelled. "Sarah, please carry on."

Sarah nodded slowly. She had already seen some of the writing below and her stomach was churning with dread. "Rule one: no escape. You can't leave, plain and simple. Try to escape and you won't like what you find. Rule two: make what you have last. Whatever food and water you currently find in the house is all that you will be provided with during your stay. No more will be given to you under any circumstances. Rule three: when the music stops, someone must die. The music you can all hear in the background will cease between eleven o'clock PM and midnight, and it is illustrated on the clock face as the red area between twenty-three and twenty-four. When this happens, someone must die. Suicides are acceptable. Failure to comply with this rule will result in everyone's death. Rule four: only one, and only when the music stops! One death, and only one death, must occur in the allotted time between eleven o'clock PM and midnight. Again, failure to comply with this rule will result in everyone's death. Deaths from accidents, injury, dehydration, etc.

count towards this rule, so play it safe and take heed of rule two! We hope you have a pleasant stay, and don't forget: *Redemption is the key to escape.*"

"What the fuck..." Lucky said, processing the information.

"One must die, one way out, one must die, one way out!" the Wreck chanted from across the room, rocking back and forth on a wooden chair with his head between his knees.

"Oh my god, this is like a nightmare!" Carl whimpered. "I don't want to die!"

"We need to find a way out, I need to get back to my daughters as soon as possible!" Melanie said frantically.

"We've been locked in here to kill each other," Komo said shakily. "There's not going to be an easy way out."

"You don't know that for sure!" Melanie replied.

"Komo's right," Jacob said calmly and firmly. "Whoever put us in here had the resources to drug and kidnap twelve people, and then brick up all the exits before we awoke. They wouldn't have made it easy for us to get out. That being said, it doesn't mean that it's completely impossible for us to break out. Every fortress has its weak spots."

"The kid's right," Mitchell said gruffly. "So we stick to the original plan and go through this place with a fine tooth comb."

"*Kid?*" Jacob said with a scoff. "I'm a man. Maybe not a hulky Neanderthal like you, but a man nonetheless."

Mitchell chuckled. "If you say so, *kid.*"

"Calm it, guys," Lucas said. "They want us to tear each other apart, so we need to try and stay on the same side."

"Exactly," Sarah agreed. "Let's just stay focused on getting out."

"What if it does come to... you know," Carl hedged. "One of us dying?"

"We could just kill the Wreck," Melanie said heartlessly.

"Leave him alone," Mitchell said harshly. "He probably can't help the way he is."

"So the muscle-head has a heart after all," Jacob said snidely.

Mitchell scowled back but then remembered something. "My little brother, he was-"

"Retarded?" Jacob interrupted.

"Different," Mitchell finished with a tone that oozed hatred.

"Calm, guys, remember?" Sarah said, trying to diffuse the situation. "No one's going to die. It's not going to come to that because we're not going to let it come to that, okay?"

Jacob and Mitchell nodded their heads but the tension still hung in the air.

"Let's get searching before someone gets hurt," Komo said before leaving the room.

Jessica laughed. "I bet people are having a great time watching this. Come on, Jack, let's see if we can find any hidden cameras." She took the handsome man by the hand and led him away.

"How does it feel holding the hand of someone famous, then?" Jack asked her in a flirtatious tone as they left the room.

"We're both famous now, silly," she replied with a giggle.

"Those two are idiots," Jacob said coldly.

"That we can agree on," Mitchell said.

"What if they're in on it?" Lucky Leo asked suspiciously.

"That kind of thinking is only going to make matters worse," Lucas replied firmly. "Any one of us could be a potential enemy when you start going down that road."

Sarah was impressed at how well Lucas was handling the situation. She still had butterflies in her stomach from reading the ghastly 'house rules' and was trying to put a brave face on, but in reality she was more afraid than she'd ever been in her whole life.

The group split up and began searching. Sarah stuck with Lucas, as his calm and level-headed demeanour put her at ease, and together they gave themselves a room-by-room tour of the house that was now their prison.

The hallway outside of the living and dining room had beige wallpaper with a slight brown aged tint to it, worn brown carpet, a wooden staircase to the first floor, and a disturbingly thick metal door with a stiff letterbox. Komo was on her knees beside the door, feeling its fixings and hinges with her hands as if some sort of secret switch would be revealed to her.

On the opposite side of the house to the living and dining room was a parlour. Its walls were decorated with a peaceful light blue and cream wallpaper, and it had a small dark blue sofa and two armchairs arranged around another glass coffee table. A pool table was in the centre of the room, several tall wooden bookshelves stood along the walls loaded with old dusty books, and there was a small black iron stove with a copper kettle on the top of it. Leo was flicking through a deck of cards which he had found amongst some board games, checking to see if it was a complete set.

The kitchen was at the far end of the house. Its walls were painted white although they were stained in places with yellow and brown patches, and the floor was chequered black and white lino. There was a working oven and refrigerator, a big sink, a large cupboard, worktops with built-in drawers, kitchen cabinets, a dark wooden door that led to the basement, and another sturdy metal door blocking any escape. In the middle of the room was a shiny black island countertop with another large sink, and it looked odd having something so modern amongst the older decor. Dan and Melanie were taking inventory of the supplies when Sarah and Lucas passed through.

A stiff wooden door led down to the dingy basement, where one solitary hanging light bulb illuminated the bare walls. Aside from a wooden workbench and big old-fashioned iron boiler, most of the room was dominated by clutter, firewood, coal, and cylindrical metal containers of various chemicals and oils. Mitchell and Jacob were searching the room together in stony silence. Jacob was kneeling on the floor looking through the various bottles and canisters, whilst Mitchell was testing the sturdiness of a sledgehammer he'd found.

Unsurprisingly, no one had made any progress in finding an escape route, so Sarah and Lucas made their way to the first floor.

There was one master bedroom with beige and gold patterned wallpaper and a dark purple carpet. The room consisted of a double bed with black sheets and pillow cases, two large wooden wardrobes, two bedside tables with matching beautiful purple glass lamps, a bookshelf, and a chest of drawers. When Lucas and Sarah entered, Jack and Jessica flinched and acted like they had been checking the vents for cameras.

Beside the bedroom was a large and thankfully modern bathroom. The floor was tiled with almost reflective black tiles, and the walls were painted creamy white. There was a shiny white bathtub big enough for two, a clean white toilet, a spotless sink, and an overhead mirrored cabinet complete with toothpaste and toothbrushes. There was also an airing cupboard which contained a working electric boiler, and was stocked with fresh flannels, towels, toiletries, and cleaning products. Carl was running the taps, and warm but slightly discoloured water was flowing from them.

"Looks like we won't be drinking that in a hurry," Sarah said dryly.

"I keep hoping it's going to clear up," Carl said, watching the water sadly.

"At least we can have a wash," Lucas said, before they left to look in the other rooms.

On the other side of the hallway there was a spare bedroom that had a double bed with light brown sheets, and a children's bedroom with two single beds, one with red sheets and the other with blue.

But one thing remained consistent throughout what they'd seen of the house; there was no way out. Every window was bricked up.

Sarah and Lucas jumped when they heard a smashing noise from downstairs. Sarah dropped the teddy bear she had been inspecting in the children's bedroom, and Lucas almost sent a toy car flying. The first crashing sound was followed by another, and then another, and then the lights began to flicker.

"Let's get down stairs quickly," Lucas suggested.

Sarah nodded and they left the bedroom.

By the time they got to the hallway, some of the others were also making their way down the stairs. Then the lights went off.

Jessica gasped and Carl whimpered in the pitch darkness, amid the sound of the cheesy background melody.

"Everyone just stay still," Jack said confidently.

"I can't see a thing!" Jessica cried.

"Oh god, we're all going to die!" Carl whimpered.

"Quiet!" Jack said harshly.

The banging from the ground floor stopped, and the lights flickered on and off before once again regaining their constant glow.

"Fuck it!" they heard Mitchell shout from downstairs.

Everyone reconvened in the living room where the Wreck was still rocking back and forth at the dining table. "No way out, no way out," he whispered to himself.

Mitchell had been taking the sledgehammer to random walls around the ground floor. The occasional section of wall had been dented inwards by his heavy blows, but at best all it had done was torn some wallpaper and chipped away some plasterboard.

"It's like the fucking walls are reinforced!" Mitchell said angrily. He smashed the sledgehammer into another patch of wall in the living room, and once again merely dented it. The lights turned off for almost a minute before turning back on again.

"Will you stop that?!" Jacob said angrily. "Do you want to be trapped here in total darkness, you blustering fool?"

"Do you want to be trapped in here full-stop?" Mitchell replied. "I'm trying to get us out of here, you little shit!"

"Try the window," Lucky Leo suggested.

"What if it goes dark again?" Carl said fearfully.

"There's only one way to find out," Komo said bravely.

Mitchell took the hammer over to the bricked-up window on the short side of the wall closest to the television and sofa. He got in position and swung it as hard as he could at the brickwork. The blow was so hard that it hurt his arms, and the only thing it achieved was a tiny bit of cosmetic damage. Luckily for the trapped twelve, the lights remained on.

Jacob laughed. "Maybe you're not as strong as you look, *big guy*."

"Do you want to try?" Mitchell asked aggressively.

"Actually, I do," Jacob said, saving face. He took the hammer and tried with all of his might to show Mitchell up, but all he achieved was a tiny chip in the brickwork and severe arm pain.

Mitchell laughed. "Leave it to the men," he said insultingly as he reclaimed the sledgehammer.

"Maybe if we take in turns we can eventually get through," Lucas said, trying to keep the group positive.

"We want to be quick about it," Melanie said miserably. "There's only enough bread and bottled water to last us a week at most. Apart from that, there are a few snacks and..."

"Booze!" Dan said happily, showing a bottle of rum in one hand and a bottle of whiskey in the other. "Plenty of drink stashed up, thank god!"

"That might not be a good idea," Sarah said apprehensively.

"If we start drinking too much alcohol we'll end up drinking more water," Jacob said intellectually.

Dan laughed and then took a long swig from the bottle of rum.

"You won't be getting any more water," Mitchell warned.

Dan shrugged. "Whatever. As long as I've got this, I'll be fine."

"Oh, I want a drink too," Jessica said happily.

"Me too, might cure my headache," Jack agreed.

"Snap, I'm in," Leo said.

"I don't think that getting drunk is a good idea," Lucas said, unimpressed. "Let's discuss what we've found first, while we're all together."

"Who the hell put you in charge?" Dan challenged.

Melanie agreed with Dan. "You are throwing around orders a lot. I don't like it."

"He's only trying to help," Sarah said defensively.

"I see..." Melanie said, throwing her a filthy look. "Of course you would side with him."

"What's that supposed to mean?" Sarah said sharply. The old woman was making her angry.

"You know what she means," Dan said with a chuckle and a hiccup.

"This really isn't helping," Komo cut in. "Lucas is right."

"If you don't snap out of it and work with us," Mitchell began, "then you two will be the first if it comes to it."

"The quicker we talk, the quicker we drink," Jack said, nudging Melanie playfully.

"Don't touch me!" she snapped back.

"Your loss, honey," Jack chuckled.

"I'd never talk to you like that," Jessica said dreamily.

Sarah put her fingers into her mouth and whistled sharply until the room was quiet.

"There's water coming from the taps in the bathroom but it's probably not drinkable," Carl said quietly, trying to be helpful. "The central heating works so I put it on."

"I managed to get the letterbox open," Komo said. "A little bit, at least. All I could see was black, though. On a good note, there's a keyhole on the metal door in the kitchen so I'm going to try to pick that."

"I stoked up the boiler in the basement to help warm this place up a bit," Jacob added. "With the heating on too it should at least be cosy while we try to escape."

"The house seems to be a weird mix of old and modern," said Sarah. "If we keep looking through everything we might find a clue as to who's trapped us in here."

"Good work, detective Sarah," Dan said jokingly, before having a big swig of whisky. "I'll try and find you a magnifying glass–"

"Jessica's got some news," Jack cut the heavy drinker off smugly. "Tell 'em, hun."

Jessica smiled. "I don't want to say I told you so, but... I found some cameras!"

"Where?" Lucas asked.

"If you look in the vents hard enough you can just about make them out," she beamed. "We're on television!"

"So you can go ahead and chill out a bit," Jack added coolly.

Mitchell shook his head disappointedly. "You know some nut-job could have put them in there to watch, a nut-job that wants us to kill each other, so why the fuck do you think we're on television?"

Jessica shrugged. "Call it women's intuition. And don't be so paranoid, it's a turn-off."

Melanie glared around the room. "I don't want to be watched, either way. We should break them."

"It's *we* now, is it?" Sarah asked dryly.

"I need to be at home with my girls," Melanie said, suddenly taking on a softer tone. "Not here, and definitely not as entertainment for an audience or a psychopath!"

"I'm going to keep trying the window," Mitchell said, "but there's more stuff in the basement that could get the vents open, if someone else wants to handle that."

"Well, *we're* not," Jessica said in a stroppy voice. "Me and Jack want to be famous. Come on, let's hit the bar," she said leaving the room with Jack, while Dan followed them merrily.

"Sorry, guys," Leo said remorsefully. "I'm going to try my luck with the drink." He followed after the others.

"I'll destroy the cameras," Jacob said. "Doesn't make sense to have our captors viewing our escape attempts."

"I'll help you," Melanie said thankfully.

"I'll take it in turns with the sledgehammer," Lucas said to Mitchell.

"Thanks," the big man said gratefully. "It takes it out of your arms more than it should."

"Me and Carl will have a proper dig around, then," Sarah said. "Take it easy if you can, though; it might be whatever they've drugged us with that's tiring you out so quickly."

The day passed on uneventfully and unproductively. Jacob and Melanie were unable to remove any of the vent grills, and every attempt caused the lights to flicker and dim until they stopped. Lucas and Mitchell knackered themselves out inflicting as much damage as they could on the front living room window, and despite their best efforts they were still a long way off breaking through. Carl and Sarah found nothing to shed light on their incarceration, and Komo kept trying to pick the lock on the kitchen door, while the others drank heavily and played poker and pool. As the twenty-third hour on the strange clock drew closer, all twelve residents met in the living room, and even the more sensible members of the group had resorted to a few alcoholic beverages in anticipation of what would happen next. As the clock's hand ticked over to the beginning of the red section, the strange music stopped and the Wreck began sobbing in the corner away from the others.

"Thank fuck," Jack began, "that stupid music has finally finished."

"According to the rules, that's not a good thing," Komo warned.

"Chill out," Jessica said dismissively. "It's not like anything is going to happen. It just makes good viewing."

"We should be careful," Mitchell said. "We don't know what's going to happen if we don't act."

"It's important that we all stay calm and don't do anything reckless," Lucas said softly.

"Exactly," Sarah agreed. "Just because they want us to do something awful doesn't mean we have to."

"Oh my god." Jessica faked a yawn. "You people are putting me to sleep. I'm going to go relax upstairs."

"I think I'll do the same," Jack said with a cheeky smile.

"Have a good *rest!*" Dan giggled as he staggered about the room with a fresh bottle of vodka in his hand.

Jessica and Jack left the room and ran up the stairs, and no one in the group was under the illusion that the two would actually be resting.

Time in the last hour of the day passed slowly. The group tried to keep themselves busy with small talk and card games, but try as they might, they were unable to quench the anxious tension amongst them.

"So…" Carl began in a shaky voice. He was sat on the sofa beside Melanie, watching as the hour hand slithered closer to midnight. "You have two daughters?"

"Yes, Caroline and Susanna," Melanie replied sadly. "It's hard to remember much about them, but I know I've got to get out of here and get back to them. They'll be worried sick!"

"I always wanted kids," Carl said sadly, "but I never had the chance. Now it looks like I never will."

The door to the living room burst open. "Bloody good job, too!" Jessica said angrily, bursting in and slamming a brown folder onto the coffee table.

Jack entered, hot on her heels. "We found this under the pillow in the main bedroom."

"Oh yeah?" Dan laughed. "Before or after the action?"

"Shut up, you horrible old man," Jessica hissed, out of character. "Carl is a paedophile!"

"What?!" Carl exclaimed. "No, I'm not! Why would you say that?"

Melanie edged away and stared daggers at him.

"The evidence is in that folder," Jack said severely.

Carl reached for it, but Melanie beat him to it. She snatched it off the table and flicked through the contents. "Police reports, several police reports – all confirming it!" She threw the folder at Carl and the papers burst out all around him.

Everyone in the room, with the exception of the Wreck, took a page or two and studied them intently.

"It's not true," Carl pleaded. "It's not true, I'm telling you!"

"It's a fucking police report, you pervert!" Jessica yelled.

"If anyone should die, it should be you," Jack said harshly.

Melanie got up and stormed out of the room without saying a word. The mood amongst the group had turned from sour to murderous in the blink of an eye.

"It's a lie, it's a lie!" Carl sobbed, sounding like the Wreck.

"Wait, everybody wait!" Sarah shouted as they began hurling insults towards Carl.

"There's no way to tell if these are real or not!" Lucas reasoned.

"Are you calling me a liar?!" Jessica screamed.

"Everyone calm the fuck down!" Mitchell barked, and the group fell silent.

"I'm with them," Jacob said, gesturing to Lucas and Sarah after the short spell of quiet. "There's no way to know for sure, and it's too convenient seeing as how we're supposed to be murdering each other."

The rest of the group begrudgingly agreed, but they did not look at Carl with anything less than contempt. Then the hour hand ticked over to midnight, and white cloudy gas began pouring out of the vents.

"Shit, that's some powerful stuff!" Jacob choked, covering his mouth and nose. "We'll be dead in minutes if we don't do something!"

"Then what do we do?" Leo spluttered. The fumes were making his eyes water and his throat burn.

Fear and panic gripped the group as they began coughing and spluttering violently. No one knew what to do. In a flash of motion Melanie stormed back into the room, yanked Carl's head back by his hair, and ran a sharp kitchen knife across his neck. The gas stopped immediately. Jessica screamed and hugged Jack tightly as the blood spilled from Carl's mortal wound, and his body slumped forward onto the carpet. The music started once again.

DAY 2

Sleep did not come easy for anyone that night, especially after the house had delivered them some troubling mail, but eventually the eleven residents fell into an uneasy slumber.

After Melanie had killed Carl, the letterbox had clanked over and over, and laying on the floor were easily a dozen identical brown folders. Each of the folders classified Carl as a different form of criminal, ranging from a petty thief all the way up to drug cartel leader, and each one of the folders completely contradicted the others. As Carl's blood oozed over the carpet, Melanie panted furiously and dropped her knife but remained as still as a statue as she stared at her victim. Jack took the distraught Jessica upstairs, and the others looked through the ridiculous reports in horrified awe. A piece of folded plain paper slid out of the letterbox, and Komo began banging on the cold metal.

"Let us out!" she screamed. "Let us out!"

Sarah picked up the paper and unfolded it. In large red letters, it confirmed what they had all feared, and she read the bad news aloud. *"Sorry, I might have lied."*

Melanie was standing in the doorway and she shook her head. "I don't care what it says, or those other reports. I did what I had to." And with that, she went upstairs and slammed the spare bedroom door shut.

"I'll put the body down in the basement," Mitchell had said coldly before leaving.

"He's going to be trouble if this is how it's going to go down," Jacob whispered. "He doesn't even seem to care."

"Neither do you," Komo said suspiciously.

When Sarah thought about it, they were all handling the events rather well considering they had seen someone's throat cut right in front of them. Only Jessica had acted truly distraught, and now she could be faintly heard over the music, giggling and chatting away to Jack in the master bedroom.

"We'll get through this," Lucas said to them. "I promise you all that we'll get out of here."

But his words rang hollow. They all knew that if they couldn't make their way through the unnaturally strong bricks in less than twenty-four hours, another one of the group would die.

Sarah and Lucas took the children's bedroom while they still could. It was selfish, but the others didn't seem to be in a hurry to hit the hay. They lay on the single beds in the pitch black, Sarah took the one with red sheets and Lucas chose the blue. They didn't say a word and listened to the eerie music until sleep finally came.

Her dreams were of pain and anguish once more. Her sister's children laughed madly amongst blood red clouds. The image shattered like broken glass, and in front of a black abyss was her sister's husband smiling at Sarah lovingly. He was hers.

"Wake up, Sarah," Lucas said frantically. "Wake up!"

Sarah opened her eyes to see Lucas kneeling over her, his hands placed gently on her shoulders. "What's wrong?" For a moment she wondered if she'd dreamt the House of Twelve too, until she registered the never-ending creepy music.

Lucas got off her and seemed embarrassed. "I was worried you were having a fit," he said, looking at her with concern. "You were shaking and screaming 'he's mine' over and over, but it must have just been a bad dream."

"Darren," Sarah murmured.

"Your other half?"

"I..." Sarah tried to remember, but it gave her a terrible headache. "I don't know. So we're still here?"

"Yeah, not a nightmare unfortunately," Lucas said grimly.

"We need to get out of here before anyone else dies," Sarah said, remembering the previous night's grim murder.

They went downstairs to find Melanie kitted out in an apron and rubber gloves, scrubbing the living room carpet with a variety of cleaning products.

"What?" she asked them aggressively when she caught them looking. "Do you want to sit around in someone else's blood?"

Sarah and Lucas said nothing, but instead made their way to the kitchen. The smell of toast hit their noses before they reached the door and it made their stomachs rumble with hunger. The others were standing around drinking bottled water and eating their breakfasts, and no one said anything as Sarah and Lucas made some of their own.

"We need to get out of here," Leo said sleepily.

"Willing to help now?" Mitchell asked coarsely.

Lucky Leo nodded guiltily.

Jack and Jessica looked around at the group with a slight hint of regret in their eyes, but didn't offer their services.

"So we know whoever's done this is going to attempt to force us against each other," Lucas began, "but it's important that we don't play into their trap like last night."

"If Carl didn't die then all of us would've done," Jacob said coldly. "I mean, it's unfortunate, but it couldn't be helped."

"Remember that when it's your turn," Komo said, equally as cold.

"My turn?" Jacob said, offended. "You said you'd open that lock for us. Maybe you should go next for failing us."

"Maybe you should go next for being a dick," Mitchell said with a smirk.

Jacob looked at him evilly. "Watch your tone-"

"Or what?" Mitchell interrupted. "What are you going to do?"

"Pack it in," Sarah chided.

Dan wandered in looking like death warmed over. He said nothing as he grabbed a bottle of water and drank it all, before reaching for another.

"That's enough!" Mitchell roared.

Dan shrugged. "Fuck off, I'm thirsty."

"You should have thought about that before you drank yourself silly," Komo said.

"Oh, shut your trap, you little bitch," Dan snapped.

Mitchell faced up to him. "Water's on ration. Deal with it and get out."

"Fine, fine!" Dan shouted. He grabbed a fresh bottle of rum and waved it around to the room. "I'll have more of this, then!"

"You're going to make yourself even thirstier," Sarah warned.

"Shut the hell up, don't tell me how to live my fucking life!" Dan yelled madly.

Before anyone could say anything more, Dan stormed out of the room.

"This is getting out of hand fast," Komo said.

"Best you get that lock open, then," Jacob snarled, before heading down to the basement.

The day passed by quickly, and like their first escape efforts it appeared to be in vain. Leo and even Sarah helped with hammering at the front window, but it seemed futile. That was until Komo began making progress with the kitchen door. Even Melanie gave up her obsessive cleaning and came to watch. Mitchell kept a close eye on Dan, who had already begun eating and drinking more than his fair share earlier that day when left unattended.

"Come on, come on..." Komo spoke to herself as she poked, prodded, and twisted an unwound metal clothes hanger and a small kitchen knife into the large old-fashioned lock.

Everyone looked on in anticipation of their escape. Mitchell held the sledgehammer ready to strike and others armed themselves with what they could, just in case their captors showed themselves. Jessica gasped as the lock clicked open.

"Help me pry it open," Komo said happily.

Lucas and Leo were closest, and they quickly came to Komo's aid. They strained their fingers on the edge of the thick metal door until it finally began to give way. As soon as they were able, they got their hands around the edge of the door and yanked it open.

"No," Lucas gasped.

"Fuck, fuck, fuck!" Komo screamed.

The other side of the door was completely bricked up. Painted in big red letters across it was: No way out... sorry.

"Just great," Jacob muttered sarcastically, as he made his way back down to the basement to be alone.

Komo was distraught. "What the hell do we do now?"

"We get through the window," Lucas said, trying his best to remain positive.

Melanie said nothing and went back to her cleaning, and Dan slunk off with more booze.

"I'm going to take a bath," Jessica said uncaringly. "I feel gross." With that, she casually walked away.

Lucas put his hand on Komo's shoulder, who was still clearly distressed, and he tried reassuring her. When it didn't work, he tried changing the subject. "Do you remember where you learnt to pick locks?"

"Not really," she said, trying to force her memory to return. "But I think I was a thief. I dreamt about stealing stuff last night," she remarked nonchalantly.

"Oh..." Lucas said, not really knowing what to say in response. "I dreamt about my Dad. Can't recall much of it, though."

"Maybe our memories are coming back to us," Komo pondered.

"No memories, clean slate, no memories, clean slate," The Wreck said plodding into the kitchen, grabbing some water and plain bread, and then plodding out in the same dazed state.

"Shame about the door, huh?" Jack said to Sarah, and he moved quite close to her side.

"Yeah," Sarah said, moving away slightly.

"Could I get you a drink?" he asked pleasantly. "To help wash down the bad news?"

"No, thank you," Sarah said abrasively. "I'm trying to help get us all out of here."

Jack smirked. "We're not getting out of here, so we might as well make the most of what life we have left. You know, you'd be really attractive if you just lightened up a bit," he added with a wink.

Sarah cringed. "Great, thanks," she said sarcastically. "I'd stick with Jessica if I were you."

Lucas approached them and Jack quickly departed. "You alright?" he asked, sensing her angst.

She shook her head. "Something's not right here."

"You mean apart from being bricked up in this fucking house?" Mitchell said gruffly.

"Yeah. I mean with them," Sarah said, implying the others. "They're just... not right."

"I know what you mean," Leo agreed. "I was with them most of yesterday and it's like this stuff just doesn't faze them."

"Maybe there's something wrong with all of us," Komo mused. "Carl died yesterday and we're not that shaken up about it. Melanie seemed distressed by what she did, but then she's not afraid to start scrubbing away at his blood for most of the day."

"It's because survival comes first," Mitchell said sternly. "Our instincts are starting to take over, and that's why we're moving on so fast. When we're out of here... that's when it will hit us, and it will probably hit us hard."

"Maybe," Sarah replied. "But that doesn't explain the behaviour of the ones who aren't concerned about getting out."

"I bet they're really concerned," Mitchell challenged. "But they've already given up because they're weak. They know it and they can't face it, and it's scrambled their brains up a bit."

"Whatever the case, we should stay cautious but do our best to keep the group together," Lucas said, being as diplomatic as ever. "We've got better odds of breaking out if we're all on the same side."

Mitchell grunted; he was bored of debating. "Let's get through this window and worry about the rest later."

The others agreed, and they went back to the living room to begin the arduous process of chipping away at the brickwork. As they left, Dan snuck back in.

Sarah, Lucas, Leo, Mitchell, and Komo worked for as long as they could before tiring too much to continue. They had begun to wear away the surface of the centre brickwork, but the horrid realisation that they wouldn't break through that day washed over them with every passing hour. They headed back to the kitchen just as the clock ticked over to twenty-three and the music stopped. They mainly wanted a quick snack and drink, as they had worked most of the day, but they also wanted to talk over the unpleasant and difficult decision that would have to be made in the next sixty minutes.

As soon as they walked through the kitchen door, each one of them knew on some level what was going to happen. Dan was passed out in the corner surrounded by a collection of empty water bottles, plastic packaging and wrappers, and a wide variety of alcohol. He had raided the supplies in their absence.

"You stupid alcoholic son of a bitch!" Mitchell roared.

Lucas tried to grab his arm as he lunged towards Dan, but was unable to hold the hulking man back. Dan's eyes opened suddenly, and without a moment of hesitation he smashed a glass bottle against Mitchell's head. The heavy drinker smiled for a second, before he realised that the attack had merely angered the raging brute. Blood trickled down Mitchell's face as he chased Dan around the ground floor of the house. Others shouted and followed, but their words and actions were lost to the pair of them in a haze of bloodlust and adrenaline. The alcoholic was quick on his feet and deftly dodged out of the way every time Mitchell attempted to stop him. Dan looked back as he entered into the living room for another circuit, only to trip on Melanie who was still scrubbing the space on the floor where her victim had bled out. He tumbled over ungracefully, and Melanie scowled and returned to her cleaning.

"I've got you now, you piece of shit!" Mitchell said, kneeling on Dan's shoulders and grabbing him around the throat.

"Wait," Dan gasped, struggling for breath.

The rest of the group looked on helplessly as Mitchell strangled Dan to death. The music began to play once again.

DAY 3

After Mitchell had dropped Dan's lifeless form, Jacob had been the first to speak up. "Care to explain that *little* outburst?"

"He was making his way through our supplies," Mitchell panted. "I did us all a favour."

"Get that body out of here," Melanie said angrily. "Can't you see that I'm trying to clean?"

"At least I didn't spill blood everywhere like you did," Mitchell growled back.

"I'm cleaning it up, okay?!" Melanie screamed.

"What gives you the right to decide who lives and dies?" Jacob said aggressively to Mitchell.

"He was eating what little food and water we have left. Unless you feel like starving until we get the fuck out of here?" Mitchell snapped back.

"You don't get to boss us around or make those kinds of calls, regardless of what he did," Jacob retorted.

"Well, I think you were too busy jacking-off in the basement at the time," Mitchell snarled. "Next time, I'll ask."

"So you've already decided that you're going to kill another one of us?" Jacob said. "I warned the others about you and it looks like I was right," he said to the room, before storming off up the stairs.

"Little shit wants to watch his tone around me..." Mitchell grumbled to himself, as he dragged Dan's lifeless corpse down to the basement.

After countless hours of lying in the pitch darkness and trying to tune out the irritating music, Sarah finally drifted off, but her dreams were hardly a pleasant escape from her prison.

They started off content enough. She was walking down a busy street, laughing and joking with the man she thought was called Darren. He was younger though, and when Sarah passed by a shop window she saw that she appeared to be more youthful also. Then the sun disappeared, the sky faded into a pure black surface, and the buildings joined together until they were one solid wall around the horizon, enclosing her on all sides. Darren ran into the distance and disappeared. Sarah ran after him – she needed him back – but it was no use. He was gone. Slowly but surely the towering walls began to move, and Sarah could do nothing but watch helplessly as the cityscape crawled inwards towards her. She tried opening doors as they moved along, but they were all locked. She tried to smash a big shop window, but when it shattered the interior disappeared along with the glass. All that was left was a brick wall with 'No way out, sorry!' written on it in fresh dripping blood. Suddenly she was standing in a house she'd never seen before, similar to the so-called House of Twelve, but there was no roof; just darkness.

"Dad, wake up!" someone called from a distance.

Sarah looked around wildly for where the voice had originated from, but she was all alone. She heard the shouting again but it was overshadowed by the cheesy background music that seemed to seep out of the walls. It grew louder and louder until she had to put her hands over her ears to dampen the deafening racket. A shadow began stretching across the house interior, and when she looked up Sarah saw a gigantic beautiful blonde woman staring down at her with an evil smirk upon her face. It was her sister.

"Dad!" Lucas screamed, waking Sarah from her nightmare.

Even though Sarah was sleepy and extremely disorientated from her nightmare, she quickly got out of bed and moved to Lucas' side. She nudged him gently at first, and then harder when he didn't immediately wake from his night terror. Eventually his eyes opened, and he looked up at Sarah with dread before fully snapping out of it.

"You okay?" Sarah asked, concerned for him. "Looks like it was my turn to save you from the bad dreams today."

Lucas nodded, still shaking. "Yeah, thanks. It was so real. My Dad, he was dead and wouldn't wake up. It was horrible."

"Mine wasn't nice either," Sarah said. The thought of her sister's face made her blood boil. "My sister isn't very nice. I wonder if she's why I'm here," she said, more to herself than to Lucas.

"You think your sister would put you through all this?" Lucas asked in shock.

Sarah couldn't exactly remember, but she nodded anyway. "Yes. Yes, I think she would."

"Maybe we've upset the wrong people and this is some sort of sick punishment," Lucas guessed unhappily.

"But we don't know each other. Surely we'd recognise each other a little bit, it would be too much of a coincidence if we were all somehow connected through the wrong people. Wouldn't it?"

"I suppose so," Lucas said dozily. "I'd like to know who's done this to us. I'm sure Mitchell will enjoy a face-to-face meeting with them when we get out of here."

"It's bad, but I wouldn't mind seeing him pull a repeat of last night on the bastards who put us in here," Sarah admitted.

"I can't believe he killed Dan," Lucas said sadly. "We need to get out of here before there are more deaths."

"With the way it's going with the window, we'll be lucky," Sarah said, facing up to the fact that more bloodshed was sure to follow. "It's ridiculously strong."

"It's not right, bricks aren't meant to be that tough," Lucas said musingly. "I keep wondering if this is just a nightmare. Something just doesn't feel right about this – apart from the obvious, I mean."

"I know what you mean," Sarah said, looking around at the children's bedroom. She couldn't place it, but something didn't *feel* right.

The day dragged on awfully. With the food and water rationed to the extreme, the people working at escape were thirsty and hungry as they smashed the hammer into the barely unflinching bricks.

Mitchell hardly spoke. After killing Dan, he had taken a much darker demeanour and it was almost frightening to be around the hulking man.

Melanie ran a bath and spent most of the day beside the bathtub, running her hands back and forth through the slightly discoloured water, deep in thought.

Jessica and Jack were as maddeningly unaffected as usual. The two played pool, drank moderately, and played cards with Leo when he was resting from his duties at the window.

Jacob popped up from time to time but spent most of the day down in the basement. What he was doing down there beside the bodies of Carl and Dan, no one knew, but they all had bigger concerns to deal with.

Komo inspected the vents more closely on her down time, and thought she might have found one in the parlour that didn't interfere with the lights like the others strangely did.

All the while, the Wreck rocked back and forth by the secure metal front door, whispering cryptic messages and crying.

While Komo was having another look in the parlour, she was approached by Jack.

"So, what are you up to?" he asked casually.

"Trying to help the group out," she replied flatly. "Unlike you."

"I know a lost cause when I see one," Jack said coolly. "Is it so bad to want to make the best of what little time we have left?"

"Does that mean you'll be killing yourself tonight, then?" Komo asked, looking unimpressed.

"That's not exactly what I had in mind," Jack said, closing into her personal space.

"Whoa, whoa!" Komo said, pushing him away. "Back the fuck off."

Jack smirked, but backed off and left the room. He looked back and gave her a longing grin that made her skin crawl.

"You like him?" Jessica asked from behind her, making Komo jump. "It's okay if you do, but he's a bit of an asshole. I'd stay away if I were you."

"I don't like him," Komo said, feeling flustered. Her heart was still beating heavily from the shock, and it made her voice tremor to the point where her statement didn't sound believable. "You don't seem to mind him too much, though; you're fucking him every night."

"Oh, I don't let him sleep with me. I just tease him a bit," Jessica said, staring through Komo with glazed-over eyes. "Men only want one thing, you see. All of them, no matter how decent they may seem. Pretty girls like us just can't let them have it, can we?"

"I suppose not..." Komo said. She was quite threatened by the 'real' Jessica.

"That's right, that's right... we'll keep them nice and close for now." Jessica blinked a few times, adjusted her hair, and walked away swaying her hips. "Jack? Jack! Where are you? I'm lonely and bored," she called as she left.

"Fucking weirdos," Komo muttered.

As the day drew to a close, everyone apart from Jessica, Jack, and the Wreck met in the kitchen. According to the strange clock on the living room mantelpiece it was around half ten in the evening.

Jacob was already standing at the island with some premade drinks. "Hey everyone. I just wanted to apologise for how I've been acting, especially to you, Mitchell," Jacob said, handing him a drink.

"What is it?" Mitchell asked suspiciously.

"Just some vodka," Jacob replied with a smile. "I thought as it's getting close to 'that time' we could all use a stiff drink."

"Well, thanks," Mitchell said awkwardly. "Sorry for how I've acted, too. This house doesn't exactly bring out the best in people, does it?"

"It certainly doesn't," Jacob agreed.

"Jacob," Komo interrupted. "I think I've found a vent grill I can get open."

"That's great," he said happily.

"Well," Komo continued, "could you get me some tools from the basement? A hammer and screwdriver, preferably? I just don't want to go down there... you know, with Carl and Dan."

"Say no more, I'll go and get them for you now," Jacob said helpfully.

Everyone had a light snack and a few sips of vodka before Mitchell voiced what everyone was thinking. "The bricked-up window isn't budging any time soon so we need to decide who's going next, and for the next few days."

"I say the Wreck goes next," Melanie said plainly. "He doesn't contribute or do anything productive. He won't be missed."

"Not an option," Mitchell dismissed outright.

"Why?" Melanie asked bitterly.

"He can't help the way he is," Sarah said.

"And we'd have to live with the fact that we'd killed someone innocent," Lucas added.

"No one is innocent," Melanie said coldly.

"Well, you're definitely not," Komo said in a cruel tone. "You slit Carl's throat."

"I killed a paedophile to save the rest of you ungrateful people," Melanie said defensively. "Just like how Mitchell killed a supply-raiding alcoholic. We're all just doing what needs to be done, and that's why the Wreck should be next."

"Go for him and I'll go for you," Mitchell growled.

"So you're the boss of all of us now, are you?" Melanie asked harshly.

"Maybe we should vote," Komo suggested. "There are two more unhelpful and useless people I'd put forward, especially as they both give me the serious creeps."

"Or we could draw lots?" Leo put forward. "Or we could play cards to decide?"

"Extreme poker," Komo sighed.

"I say we draw lots," Lucas said. "We put everyone's name in – *everyone's*. We pick out a name and that's that."

"It sounds like the only fair option," Sarah agreed.

"But how will we tell if it's fair or not?" Melanie asked, putting a spanner in the works. "Someone could rig it somehow."

"Well, we all write our own name on a scrap of paper and then put it in a bowl or something, and then just pull one out?" Lucas said.

"Who pulls the name out, then? Someone could look for a person that they're not fond of," Melanie said sharply.

"Seriously?" Komo sighed.

"We could get the Wreck to pick it out. He doesn't know what's going on," Sarah said, half joking and half serious.

Everyone paused as the music stopped.

"We've got one hour to figure this out," Lucky Leo said softly.

"Thanks for pointing out the obvious," Melanie snapped.

Jacob returned and handed the tools to Komo. "What have I missed, then?" he asked, taking a long drink from his vodka.

"We're deciding who's going next," Sarah said miserably.

"Best we've got is pulling out a name at random, but we're now arguing over the details," Komo said dryly.

"There must be some way we can decide that's fair and that everyone agrees on," Lucas said, trying to get back on track.

"I still think we should just vote between Jessica and Jack," Komo admitted, thinking of her earlier encounters with them.

"Maybe Komo's right," Sarah said, remembering how uncomfortable Jack had made her feel earlier in the day.

"Sarah!" Lucas chided in a disappointed tone. "I thought you were with me on this?"

"I am, Lucas," Sarah said. Upsetting him was the last thing she had intended. "But they really don't help. If anything, they do the opposite."

"I agree," Mitchell said. "It should be one of those two."

"It should be the Wreck," Melanie said with annoyance.

"Deciding shouldn't be a problem," Jacob said chirpily.

"Why is that?" Lucas asked in confusion.

"Yeah, why do you say that?" Sarah asked, not liking his tone.

"Oh, any minute now it's all going to be taken care of," Jacob said with a big smile.

Mitchell finished his vodka and smirked evilly, as though he was part of a grand revelation. "The *kid* is right. The decision has apparently been made for us, for tonight anyway."

Jacob chuckled confidently. "I took the liberty-"

"Of poisoning my drink," Mitchell interrupted.

"I'm glad you see that this is the right course of action," Jacob said, sounding impressed.

"It's not that," Mitchell said, draining the last few drops out of his glass. "I switched our glasses when you were in the basement for Komo. Just in case. Sorry, *kid.*"

"No..." Jacob said, looking fearfully down at his glass. "But how could you have known?"

"No one drops a grudge that fast," Mitchell began with a smile, "and I might have found this down in the basement last night." He pulled a newspaper clipping out of his pocket and showed it to the room. It was an incomplete article titled '*University poison killer revealed*' with a black and white picture of Jacob's face on it. "So I thought I should take your *generosity* with a pinch of salt, it looks like the house doesn't always lie," Mitchell added with a chuckle.

"You knuckle-dragging bastard!" Jacob began coughing violently and blood ran down his hands as he cupped them over his mouth. The large dose that was intended to kill Mitchell slowly (and timed accordingly with the house rules) was now tearing through his skinnier body at an alarming rate.

"You really think you could get one over on me?" Mitchell snarled to the dying young man. "You stupid little shit."

Jacob collapsed on the floor before he could utter a reply.

Mitchell chuckled menacingly as he dragged the body down into the basement.

DAY 4

Sarah was standing in a strange living room with bricked-up windows and doors. A weird clock was on the mantelpiece with its only hand pointed at twenty-three, and a body was in the far corner of the room covered by a bed sheet. Around her were ten strangers looking apprehensive, and one of them was holding a bag full of folded paper. They all took turns in taking a piece of paper until everyone had one each, and then they slowly opened them up. A wave of relief spread through the group, and then Sarah hesitantly opened hers to reveal an ominous black mark in the centre. She looked up and the group was slowly advancing towards her, their faces twisting and distorting madly. Suddenly she was being set upon by her Mother, Father, sister, Darren, their children, and other members of her family.

Sarah jolted out of bed and saw that Lucas had just done the same. "We can't even catch a break in our sleep, can we?" she panted, catching her breath.

"Doesn't look like it," Lucas said, also breathing heavily.

"Can you smell that?" Sarah asked, sniffing like an animal; she could smell cooking meat.

"Yeah, it's making me hungry," Lucas replied. "Maybe someone found some proper food."

They went downstairs and headed to the kitchen. The Wreck was huddled up by the front door repeating the phrase 'we're all dead', and with the exception of him it looked like they were the first ones to wake. They could hear the others struggling and talking in their sleep. When they got to the kitchen they found Melanie cleaning the floor obsessively, but there was no sign of any cooking being done.

"Melanie?" Lucas began. "Do you know where that smell is coming from?"

"We thought someone was cooking down here," Sarah added.

"Downstairs," Melanie muttered, not looking up from her cleaning for a moment. It looked like she hadn't slept at all.

Sarah and Lucas looked at each other, neither of them liking where the situation was going. They slowly opened the door to the basement and the smell of burning meat hit them hard. They looked down the stairs to see Mitchell mercilessly sawing the bodies of the dead into pieces on a large roll of tarpaulin, and feeding them gradually into the big old coal and wood boiler.

Sarah ran into the kitchen and threw up into the sink, to the dismay of Melanie who immediately refocused her cleaning efforts in that direction.

"Mitchell!" Lucas said, covering his mouth and trying not to gag. "What the hell are you doing?!"

Mitchell looked up from his gruesome work. He had bags under his eyes and clearly hadn't slept either. "Is it morning already?" he grumbled. "I'll be done soon, you make a start without me and I'll join you as soon as I can."

"Why are you doing... *that*?" Lucas repeated desperately.

"We can't have rotting bodies this close to our food," Mitchell said. "It's not pretty but it just needs to be done."

Lucas looked at him with an expression of pure dismay, but left the brute to his awful self-appointed duty.

"He's disposing of them before they make the place unhealthy," Lucas explained to Sarah.

"My god," Sarah gasped. "The blood and gore..." She retched at the thought.

"What's with the smell?" Komo asked, rubbing her eyes.

"Don't ask," Lucas said grimly.

Komo thought about pressing the issue, but looking at the state of Sarah she decided against it. "Are you all getting weird nightmares?"

"Every night," Sarah said, nodding her head.

"Same here unfortunately," Lucas replied.

"I was stealing some money from a bank or something," Komo said dreamily. "I'd just done this awesome hack and then all the exits bricked themselves up. I was trapped with no way out, it was awful."

"You're trapped now too, silly little slut," Melanie muttered as she was cleaning the sink.

"So because I'm young and pretty, I'm a slut?" Komo pressed.

"That, and you're an Asian," Melanie spat, not looking up from the sink.

Komo went to swing for her but Sarah grabbed her arm. "Ignore her, she's not worth it."

"Pair of whores," Melanie whispered to herself as they left the room.

"I know you're having a hard time coping but you're not helping matters here," Lucas said to her as calmly as he could.

Melanie said nothing to him in response, so he left her to her cleaning.

Everyone else began to wake up. Each of them commented on the smell, and Lucas and Sarah explained as timidly as they could that Mitchell was 'disposing' of the bodies. Lucas, Leo, and Sarah began their day's work at the window, while Komo took a dining chair from the living room and into the parlour to begin investigating the potentially loose vent grill.

Komo pried, poked, and wedged the grill, only pausing to tell Jack to go away when he tried his luck with her again. Luckily all the lights stayed on throughout her interference, and by lunchtime she had managed to remove it. Staring into the shadowy depths within the vent, she could just about make out a lens.

She went to the living room to see Sarah, Lucas, and Leo looking exhausted and resting on the sofa and armchairs, whilst a blood-splattered Mitchell hammered relentlessly into the impassable brickwork.

"I've got the grill off," Komo began, eying Mitchell's bloody attire cautiously. "If someone can give me a lift, I'll try and get the camera out. At least there'll be one less."

Mitchell stopped and handed the sledgehammer to Leo, who took his place. "Sure, let's go."

"I wonder why this one came off so easy," Lucas pondered.

"Who knows, everything about this place seems weird," Sarah said as they walked to the parlour.

Mitchell lifted Komo onto his shoulders and she reached as far as she could into the old vent. She scrunched her face up and clawed at where the camera was, and with a yank that almost sent her flying off the brutish man's shoulders, she ripped the object free. Mitchell lowered her down and they all stared in disbelief at what was in her hands.

"It's just a box!" Sarah said in shock.

"What the fuck?" Mitchell growled.

Komo turned it in her hands. It was just a small cardboard box with a lens stuck on the outside. She tore it open, and inside was an envelope addressed to Lucas in elegant writing.

"I don't like this one bit," Sarah said, afraid of what was written inside.

Lucas slowly opened and unfolded a letter that was inside the envelope. His expression was that of pure confusion as he passed it to the rest of the group to see.

"It's a Will," Komo said puzzled.

"Yeah," Lucas breathed, "my Dad's last Will and Testament."

"How did it get in here?" Mitchell asked almost accusingly.

"I really don't know, but what if...?" Lucas paused. "I dreamt that he was dead. What if he is?"

"I'm sorry," Sarah said, unsure of what to say.

"Whoever set this up probably did this to demoralise you," Komo said sadly. "I'm sorry for your loss, if that is the case."

"We've got bigger issues right now," Mitchell said coldly. "Let's get back to the brickwork."

"That's a hell of a lot of zeros, though," Komo said as she handed the Will back to Lucas. She discarded the fake camera and tried to get as much dust off of her arm as possible.

"Yeah, wow, I suppose it is," Lucas said, noticing for the first time just how much wealth was displayed on the document. He lingered behind, looking at the document before snapping out of his trance and re-joining the escape effort.

When they got back to the front of the living room, Leo lowered the hammer. "How did it go?"

"It was a fake," Mitchell said blankly as he picked up the sledgehammer and began chipping away at the brickwork again.

"Just a lens stuck to a box," Komo elaborated.

"I don't know whether to be relieved or not," Lucky Leo said, confused.

"Join the club," Sarah said miserably.

"I've got a sort of proposition for you all," Leo hedged. "About tonight."

"What do you mean?" Sarah asked.

Leo reached behind his back and pulled a revolver out of the top of his trousers. The others flinched back, worried about what would happen next.

"It's cool, I'm not going to shoot you," Leo said, trying to sound reassuring.

"Where the hell did you find that?!" Komo asked.

"Upstairs," Leo explained. "In one of the drawers in the master bedroom."

"Is it loaded?" Lucas asked cautiously.

Leo nodded. "With one bullet."

Mitchell stopped his hammering long enough to comment. "So that was your plan if someone tried to take you out?"

"That was my plan," Leo said sheepishly, "but I've got a different idea now."

"Which is?" Sarah asked, concerned.

"As you all know, I like a good gamble," Leo began, "and to be honest I can't stand this crap anymore, wondering if I'm going to be next or not. So if someone else is game, how about some Russian Roulette tonight?"

Komo chuckled, thinking he was joking. Mitchell carried on hammering and Sarah was too afraid to speak.

"I'll do it," Lucas said bravely.

"No!" Sarah gasped. "You can't be serious?!"

"It's okay," he said distantly. "At least this way you all have another day to make your way through that bloody window. I like a gamble too," he added, forcing a smile.

"Good man," Leo said, putting the gun away and patting Lucas on the back.

Sarah stared at them both in disbelief but couldn't think what to say. She was speechless from shock. Komo looked at her sadly but said nothing, before she traded places with Mitchell.

Sarah went upstairs to the bathroom. She wanted to be alone for a while, but found Melanie kneeling beside the bathtub running her hands back and forth through the water again.

"Are you getting in?" Sarah asked slightly coarsely.

"If you had children you'd know what I was going through," Melanie said bitterly.

"We're all struggling." Sarah thought about Jack and Jessica. "Well, most of us are. Just stop acting like you're the only one suffering here."

"How dare you!" Melanie shouted.

"How dare I what?" Sarah shouted back. She could feel the anger and adrenaline rising from within her, and it started to feel surprisingly good. "Get in the bath or get the fuck out!"

Melanie went to reply but met Sarah's eyes and decided otherwise, so she quickly got up and stormed past her without saying a word.

Sarah slammed the door closed, flicked the lock shut, and then burst into angry tears.

Eventually, Sarah regained her composure and re-joined the others. Jack and Jessica were standing in the hallway flirting and giggling, and she honestly felt like taking Leo's gun and ending one of the strange pair where they stood. Her foul mood was churning her stomach so badly that it physically hurt.

When the clock finally ticked over to twenty-three and the frustrating background music ceased, Leo and Lucas sat opposite each other on the dining room table. Everyone else gathered at a distance to watch what would happen, and even the Wreck peeped in through the hallway.

"Redemption is the key to escape," the Wreck muttered. "Is this redemption?" he asked himself over and over again.

Leo pushed out the cylinder of the revolver and showed Lucas the single bullet that was inside amongst the other five vacant chambers. "Care to do the honours?"

"Sure, why not?" Lucas said, taking the gun, closing it, and spinning the cylinder. "Want me to go first?"

"If you fancy," Lucky Leo said nervously.

"Please don't–" Sarah began, but Lucas already had the barrel of the gun to his temple.

The whole room held their breaths as Lucas steadied his nerves and pulled the trigger. The gun clicked and nothing happened. He exhaled with relief and passed the gun across the table to Leo.

Sarah also exhaled with relief, but she knew that her good friend could still meet his end.

Leo quickly picked up the gun, and without stopping to think he pushed it to his head and pulled the trigger. Again, nothing happened.

Lucas took the gun and slowly took his turn, knowing that the odds of his survival were decreasing every time. But again, nothing happened.

Lucky Leo was now breaking into a nervous sweat. He struggled to grasp the gun at first because his hands were so clammy, but when he did, he closed his eyes and pulled the trigger. The gun clicked and did nothing again.

Lucas took his turn quickly, knowing full well that there was a fifty-fifty chance that his death was coming, and to his immense relief the gun didn't fire.

Lucky Leo looked distraught. He hesitated before picking up the revolver. "I guess you can't win them all," he said as he closed his eyes. He put the barrel to the side of his head and slowly pulled back the trigger.

Most of the people in the room looked away, knowing what was about to happen next. They waited to hear the gunshot nervously, but Sarah was feeling strangely uplifted. She didn't want Lucas to die, even if that meant someone else having to go in his place.

The gun clicked but it didn't go off.

Leo chuckled at first and then began laughing ecstatically. He banged his fist on the table with excitement. "That's why they call me lucky!" he cheered.

"It doesn't work," Lucas sighed, feeling his heart beating in his chest.

"Now we need to figure out who's dying tonight," Mitchell said grumpily.

"It doesn't work, it doesn't work!" Lucky Leo cheered like a madman as he carried on pulling the trigger of the gun. He continued to do so as he put it to his head and pulled a comical face, imitating Lucas and himself during the course of their dreadful game.

Lucas chuckled at Leo, so relieved that neither of them had died. He was too happy to even care about who would have to die to save the rest of them that night. Then the gun fired.

Everyone flinched, yelped, or screamed as Leo's blood and brains caked the wall and what remained of his head thumped onto the wooden table. Lucas recoiled so much that he fell backwards off his chair, and as he tried to pick himself up off the floor, blood began running down the edge of the table. The music began seeping through the walls again and broke the fear-stricken silence.

DAY 5

Mitchell took the body down to the basement, whilst Melanie furiously and obsessively cleaned up the gore-stricken room. No one else had the stomach for it except for the Wreck, who continued looking on from the hallway. "That wasn't redemption, we'll have to think of a different way out," he said sadly to himself.

"I can't believe you did that!" Sarah said as she walked up the stairs with Lucas, partially relieved but also angry that he'd engaged in the crazy idea in the first place.

"I'm not sure if I'm such a good guy," he replied cryptically. "Maybe it should have been me that died tonight."

"What are you talking about?" Sarah asked. "You're one of the only people that's holding us together."

Lucas clearly went to say something, but hesitated. Instead, he wished her a goodnight and turned off the children's room light.

Sarah couldn't drift off and she sensed that Lucas was also lying awake for most of the night, but the pair didn't interact. They just stared up at the dark ceiling until they finally lapsed out of one nightmare and into another.

She was sitting in a house. Unlike the House of Twelve from her living nightmare, this one was quite pleasant, and the windows and doors were all normal. There was no sign of imprisoning brickwork, and soft warm sunlight shone into the house from the outside world.

Sarah sat alone on a comfortable white sofa opposite a large flat screen television, and stared around at the calm, peaceful surroundings. Everything was crisp and clean, expensive and well-kept, and the only thing out of place that she could see was that all the picture frames were facing down, hiding whatever pictures they held.

The horrible events in the House of Twelve seemed like another life, and instead of feeling terror and dread, her mood was that of melancholy and misery. For some reason, she couldn't bring herself to get up or even move that much. She was rooted to the spot by her own foul mood. She avoided looking out of the windows; the light and the noise coming from the outside world hurt her head and made her angry, and she almost wished that they were blocked off.

A picture floated slowly like a snowflake down from the ceiling, and came to a stop on the fancy polished wood coffee table before her. It was a picture of herself when she was younger, standing happily with her sister's husband, Darren, *before* he was her sister's husband. He had his arm around Sarah's shoulders. Quickly and coldly, without even thinking about it, Sarah slammed a long sharp knife into the picture, right into Darren's head. She immediately released her hand from the handle and recoiled back in shock. The knife wobbled side to side as the tip was firmly stuck in the table. The shock quickly dissipated, and a furious rage brewed in her stomach and chest. She didn't understand it or question it, but instead embraced it.

Sarah stormed all around the house – which she now recognised as her own – and closed the curtains, shutting out the world beyond. The noise and light still pervaded in from the outside, and the people talking and children giggling became a never-ending background din that hurt her ears. She put her hands over her ears, and something snapped inside her mind. She smashed up her furniture, destroyed ornaments, and shattered lights and lamps until the entire house was decimated. The curtains warped into brickwork, and she screamed and laughed hysterically. It felt like there were two people inside her head both fighting for control, and then she awoke.

The bedroom light was on and Lucas was already gone. Feeling groggy, she rolled out of bed and went to the bathroom. Melanie was skulking about nearby but quickly got out of the way, and Sarah slammed the bathroom door and locked it behind her. She washed her face with cold water, unconcerned about whether it was fresh or not, and stared into the mirror. As she looked into her own blue eyes, she didn't fully recognise herself. With all the focus on escaping the House of Twelve, she'd never put much effort into trying to regain her memory about her life or who she even was. Sarah wondered how much truth was hidden in her dreams amongst the seemingly random chaos. She tried to force her mind into action in an attempt to dig up her missing past, but every thought about herself or her family brought up painful emotions and awful migraines. In the end she gave up, brushed her teeth, and left the bathroom.

"You alright, hot stuff?" Jack asked flirtatiously. He was waiting outside the bathroom.

"I *was*..." Sarah said in annoyance as she tried to walk by him.

Jack blocked her path playfully. "Come on, don't be like that, Sarah. I'm only trying to be friendly."

"Get out of my way," Sarah said angrily, trying to get past.

"I said, don't be like that!" Jack snarled, grabbing her by the shoulders.

"Get the fuck off me!" Sarah shouted, as she struggled to get free.

"Jack!" Jessica called out angrily. She had popped her head out of the master bedroom to see what was happening. "What are you doing to *her*?"

Jack immediately let go. "Nothing, babe," he said smoothly. "I was just playing."

"Well, come here and *play* with me," Jessica purred seductively.

Jack gave Sarah a sly smirk before heading back to the bedroom with Jessica, and he closed the door behind him.

Sarah rushed downstairs, unsure of exactly what had happened, but either way she didn't like it. As soon as she got to the stairs she could hear the knocking sound of metal on brickwork over the god-awful background music, and she wondered just how long she had slept for. The others were hard at work trying to escape, but she went to the kitchen first.

The Wreck was sitting by the metal door that Komo had unlocked and was muttering cryptic nonsense as usual. "We're all dead, we're all dead, redemption is the way out, but how do we redeem?" he repeated over and over, only stopping to chomp on a loaf of bread.

Sarah made herself some toast and treated herself to a rare chocolate biscuit that had survived Dan's raid of the stores. She hated to admit it, but now that there were only eight prisoners stuck in the house, there was definitely more food to go around. She looked fearfully at the basement door and wondered if Mitchell had 'disposed' of un-Lucky Leo while she was asleep.

Jessica walked into the kitchen. Her red hair was slightly ruffled and she was in a state of mild undress. Her fantastic body was hard to miss.

"I thought you were *playing*?" Sarah asked bitterly as Jessica gathered some food and drink to take upstairs.

"It doesn't take much to tire him out," Jessica replied coldly. "I doubt he'd be able to fuck for very long at all. It's pathetic, really."

Sarah was shocked; she'd never heard Jessica speak like that before. "I don't understand, I thought you liked him?"

"He's a man, they're all disappointments," Jessica said, staring blankly into space. "Don't worry, I won't let him lay his hands on you again," she assured her, before twitching her head and regaining her ditzy composure.

Sarah looked on nervously as Jessica smiled playfully and took the food and drink out of the kitchen, and back upstairs to Jack. The residents were beginning to crack. Either the house was really starting to get to them, or they were just broken to begin with. The thought made Sarah's head hurt, so she tried not to think about it and ate her food.

When she went to join the others at the window she was pleased to see that they had made some decent progress. There was now a small crater shape forming in the centre, but the rest of the brickwork was remaining intact instead of crumbling and breaking as it should have been. Even the cement between the bricks was holding firm. She hoped that with a little bit more work they could create a weak spot that would allow them to destroy the rest a lot quicker.

Mitchell had fresh bloodstains on his clothing and bags under his eyes, a clear sign that he had indeed stayed up to burn Leo's remains. He was swinging the sledgehammer as hard as he could, but he was definitely too tired for the task at hand.

Komo and Lucas were sitting on the sofa trying to lose themselves in books from the parlour. They too looked worn and shattered. Sarah looked at the clock and saw that she had slept right through to the afternoon. Realising that without Leo there would be one less person helping with the hammering, she apologised thoroughly and immediately relieved Mitchell, taking his place.

"It's okay," Lucas said, forcing a smile. "You looked so peaceful, I didn't want to wake you."

"It was a weird dream," Sarah said in-between swings, "but it definitely wasn't pleasant."

"I only slept a little bit," Mitchell began dozily, "but it felt like I dreamt for a lifetime. Some people hurt my brother so I hurt them back, but I don't know if it really happened or not."

"I keep dreaming of that perfect heist," Komo said sadly. "Then a guard comes along and it all goes horrible."

"I..." Lucas hesitated. "I keep seeing my Dad falling down the stairs. Last night, the house filled with money afterwards. I think it was because we found the Will yesterday."

"I found something under my pillow in the spare bedroom this morning," Komo admitted shakily. She pulled a small photo out of her pocket. It was of a young man holding a little boy and standing with his arm around a pregnant woman.

The photo reminded Sarah of the one she saw in her dream. Her stomach churned and her eyes narrowed at the thought. "Who are they?" she tried to ask normally.

"I don't know," Komo replied, visibly confused, "but the man looks the same as the security guard out of my dreams."

"Did you look under that pillow before?" Mitchell asked cautiously. "Before last night, I mean?"

"I can't remember, but someone else might have done," Komo replied.

"I wonder if our captor really is among us," Mitchell growled, looking around suspiciously.

"I don't know about that. I just think we've all done wrong," Lucas said grimly, "and this is our punishment."

"I don't think that's the case," Sarah replied, going back to the window. "I just think we've caught some lunatic's eye, been heavily drugged, and we're in here for their sick, twisted amusement." She smashed the hammer into the wall as hard as she could, using her new-found aggression to aid in the delivery of the strike. Pain reverberated up her arms but she just didn't care.

"I thought you agreed there was something *wrong* with this place?" Lucas questioned.

"There is," Sarah said back sternly, "and as soon as we puncture through this fucking window, we'll put it *right*."

Komo gave up with the book and sat in front of the television. She began flicking through the static aimlessly, just for something to do as she waited for her turn with the sledgehammer.

Melanie had returned to cleaning up after Leo's somewhat accidental suicide. She had done a pretty good job considering, but the blood had stained the wallpaper as well as the carpet. Along with Carl's bloodstain from the first night in the house, Melanie had plenty of futile scrubbing to keep her occupied.

"Whoa, I've found a channel!" Komo said, jumping to her feet in shock.

Mitchell chuckled. "Now you're talking. You've found some porn, Komo."

Sarah stopped hammering to take a curious look. There was an attractive naked woman tied by each limb to a four-poster bed, and she was moaning out of pleasure or maybe discomfort. "Of all the things to find, Komo..."

"Maybe there are more channels we can get," Lucas said hopefully. "Any glimpse into the world outside would be a slight comfort, at least."

"Fuck that! I say leave it where it is," Mitchell said boisterously. "I want to see some action first!"

A man's face appeared on the screen. It appeared that he was adjusting the camera to get a better view of the bound woman.

"Is that Jack?" Komo asked, surprised.

"I think it is," Lucas said worriedly. Nothing that the house revealed ever seemed good.

Mitchell laughed. "That's him alright. Looks like our boy is a porn star."

"I don't know..." Sarah said. The Jack on the screen had little of his cool suave composure. Instead he had a savage, hungry look on his face, and it was a look that Sarah had seen for herself that very same day.

"Yeah," Komo said equally anxious, "I don't think this is–"

She was cut off by the Jack on the screen. "There we go, we're all set."

The girl on the bed sobbed. "Let me go, please, please!"

Jack walked away from the camera. He was naked and holding a gag, and straddled the poor girl on the bed. "What did I tell you about making a noise? You want this, you want me!" he roared demonically, striking her in the face with his fist.

"You're right, this isn't porn," Mitchell snarled. "Jack's a fucking rapist."

The Jack on the screen forced the gag on his victim and positioned himself on top of her. "There we go, see? I told you that you wanted me, you know you do. Give me a good ride and I might not hurt you again..."

Lucas turned away in disgust. "Komo, turn this off please, I think we've seen enough."

Komo tried switching off the television but the picture remained on. She tried switching channels but that didn't work either. "It won't turn off."

"Turn it down, at least!" Sarah wailed. The rape on the screen was getting louder by the second.

"Turn it off! Turn it off!" Melanie screamed with her hands over her ears. The woman was clearly close to breaking point.

"It's not working!" Komo shouted above the horrific din.

Mitchell got up and pulled the plug from the wall socket. The screen went black and the group sighed gratefully.

The Wreck wandered into the room. "Divide and conquer, one by one, dropping like flies, until we remember what we've done," he said, before walking off again.

Melanie went to say something unpleasant but met Mitchell's steely gaze, and continued scrubbing the floor and walls with a face like thunder.

Then the television came back on.

"What the fuck!" Mitchell jumped.

"That's *impossible*," Lucas muttered.

"Maybe it's got a... battery or something!" Komo shouted above the cruel rape video.

Jack and Jessica walked into the room looking amused. "Have you lot finally decided to relax a bit?" Jack asked loudly.

"I like porn, but do you have to play it that loud?" Jessica yelled playfully.

The group wordlessly parted so that Jack could see the screen, their eyes oozing malice, fear, and disgust.

"What?" Jack shouted, seeing his resemblance to the man on the screen. "Even if that is meant to be me, you know the house lies!"

"Oh, turn this horrible accusing video off. I thought you lot were finally enjoying yourselves, I should have known better!" Jessica shouted disapprovingly.

"We can't!" Mitchell roared, holding the plug socket up for them to see.

"I had your friend, too," the Jack on the screen snarled to his victim while he continued violating her roughly and relentlessly. "The one you were looking for... she wasn't good, so I had to punish her."

The girl managed to head-butt Jack on the nose, and blood spilled out over her face and chest. Jack yelped and held his face.

"You stupid, stupid... bitch!" he roared like a demon. He got off her, went off camera for a moment, and then returned with an aluminium bat. He raised it above his head and swung it downwards, right as the real-life Jack grabbed the sledgehammer and shattered the television screen with it.

The set buzzed and cackled but thankfully died out, though the group hardly noticed now. Their attention was solely fixed on Jack.

"Bloody house," Jack said angrily. "Whoever put us in here made that up to turn you guys against me."

"It didn't need to," Mitchell growled. "I was already against you."

"What can you remember?" Sarah asked angrily.

"About what?" Jack asked awkwardly.

"About your life?" Komo said aggressively. "About who you are!"

"Calm down," Lucas tried to reason, but it was obvious his heart wasn't in it anymore. "We shouldn't trust the house, but we still need to discuss this I'm afraid, Jack."

"I don't remember anything," Jack said defensively. "The lot of you should just back the fuck off and forget that ridiculous *forged* video you just saw."

"Don't worry, sweetie," Jessica said softly, taking Jack by the hand. "I don't believe it for one second." She kissed him passionately and led him out of the room.

"Jessica, you can't," Sarah said distraught.

"Not after what you've just seen," Komo interrupted hastily.

"Relax," Jessica purred. "I'll be *fine*."

Sarah continued hammering away at the wall, making up for lost time, while Komo carefully inspected the insides of the old-fashioned television set, determined to find a scientific explanation for what had happened. No one spoke about what they'd seen, but they all knew that they were leaning very close to a verdict on who would die that night.

"There's something in here," Komo said, carefully reaching around the bits of shattered glass and sharp components. "It's a locket!"

"Great," Mitchell sighed. "More mysteries yet to come..."

Komo held up a small heart-shaped silver locket, and small drops of water dripped from it. "It's wet; might explain some of the glitches."

"Yeah, because televisions turn themselves back on all the time, especially when they're not plugged in," Mitchell dismissed sarcastically.

Melanie rushed towards Komo and snatched the locket from her hands. "Where did you get this?" she snapped.

"In the TV," Komo replied.

"That's ridiculous," Melanie said furiously. "You've had it all along, haven't you? Little Asian thief-whore!"

Komo slapped Melanie as hard as she could, almost knocking the older woman off her feet and leaving a big red mark on the side of her face. "I don't tend to carry around soggy jewellery, you miserable old bat!"

Komo stormed towards Sarah and took the hammer, and for a moment the others wondered if she was about to use it as a weapon, until she began hitting the bricked-up window with her pent-up aggression.

Melanie shakily touched her face, and then opened the locket. A surprising amount of water leaked out from it. Tears welled up in her eyes, and then she ran out of the room.

Komo continued assaulting the brickwork and shouting Melanie-related insults.

When the weird clock pointed at eighteen, the workers stopped for some food. Over the cheesy background noise they could hear whining from the kitchen. Rushing into the kitchen, they found Melanie tugging at the Wreck's arm.

64

"Come on, you need to wash," Melanie said coarsely.

"I don't understand! That's not the way out, we don't need to wash," the Wreck babbled frantically between whines and squeals.

Mitchell pushed Melanie away. "Listen, lady, I don't know what your problem is but you leave him alone!"

Melanie's eyes were puffy and bloodshot. "He needs a wash, he's filthy and he needs to be cleaned!"

"Do your crazy-ass house cleaning, by all means, but stay away from the poor guy," Komo said threateningly.

Melanie looked at her angrily and then tried to grab the Wreck again. Mitchell pushed her over so hard that she fell to the floor, and without trying to get up she scuttled out of the room on all fours.

"It's okay," Mitchell said, patting the Wreck on the shoulder. "She's gone now and she won't hurt you. I promise."

"We're all gone," the Wreck replied almost lucidly. "But thank you, anyway."

Mitchell turned to the others. "I'm torn between Melanie and Jack."

"For what?" Lucas asked cautiously.

"You know exactly what I mean," Mitchell said aggressively, pointing in Lucas' face as he spoke.

After they had eaten, they carried on their work at the window. Komo couldn't find anything too unusual about the television but admitted that it was a few decades before her area of expertise, and thankfully the rest of the day passed by without any more chaotic events. When the clocked ticked over to twenty-three and the music stopped, the difficult discussion began.

"What are we going to do?" Sarah asked, already confident that she knew how the next hour would play out.

"Pick between the rapist and the crazy killer," Mitchell said flatly. "If none of you want to take care of them, I will."

"Potential rapist," Lucas reminded him.

"Is that a vote for Melanie?" Mitchell snapped.

"I..." Lucas hesitated.

"I vote Melanie," Komo said heartlessly.

"Same," Mitchell agreed.

"I vote..." Sarah began. "Do you hear that?"

There were a lot of thumping and bumping sounds coming from upstairs, and they seemed to be getting louder.

"That's ditzy and the rapist doing the dirty, most likely," Mitchell chuckled.

"She said she doesn't sleep with him," Komo said, looking slightly worried.

"They spend most of their time in the bedroom," Mitchell replied. "It's pretty obvious that they're screwing."

"He gives me the creeps, but it doesn't look like he's hurt Jessica," Sarah said. "So I vote Melanie."

"Good, then it's settled," Mitchell said as the noise from above died out. "I'll make it quick – unless you want the honours, Komo?"

"It's tempting but I'll let you handle it, thanks," Komo replied.

"What have we become?" Lucas asked miserably.

Sarah put her arm around him and gave him a little hug. "It's them or us, just remember that."

Lucas nodded sadly, and the music began playing again.

"Jessica," Sarah gasped. "It's Jack; he must have killed Jessica!"

"Then the video was right," Lucas said in shock.

"At least the next two days are covered," Mitchell said nonchalantly.

They rushed up the stairs and barged into the master bedroom. The room was completely wrecked. Torn bedding and pillow feathers littered the floor, and both lamps were smashed leaving a lone light bulb hanging from the ceiling to illuminate the room. To their great surprise, Jack was lying on the bed with his head and face bleeding. His naked body was scratched and cut, his neck was red, and his eyes stared lifelessly at the ceiling. It took a moment for them to register Jessica standing in the corner, her beautiful naked body heaving as she panted heavily, and her face was a mask of terror and fright.

"Oh, I'm so sorry!" she cried as she flung herself at Lucas. "You were all right, he tried to rape me!"

Lucas went bright red as the completely nude Jessica squeezed him tightly. "Let's get you covered up, you poor thing." He wriggled out of her grasp and handed her a blanket.

Sarah knew she should be sympathetic, but the sight of Jessica's curvaceous figure wrapped around Lucas made her stomach twist and turn with jealousy. She could feel the anger building in her chest, and she struggled to keep her mouth shut and her head from twitching.

"You're so kind," Jessica said, making little attempt to cover her private parts or even her body in general. "I'll be more helpful from now on, I promise. It was Jack's fault, he made me stay with him most of the time."

"About time," Mitchell grumbled. "We could use an extra pair of hands."

"I can't stay here tonight," Jessica directly whined to Lucas. "Stay with me in the spare bedroom, I'll feel so much safer. Please, Lucas?"

Lucas looked at Sarah longingly, but quickly turned away after sensing her anger and jealousy. "I'm sorry-" he began to Jessica.

"Oh please, please, please! I don't want to be left alone, not after what he did to me!" Jessica pleaded.

"Say what you will, but I think Jack came out worse off," Komo mumbled to Sarah.

Sarah nodded, not wanting to speak in case her emotions got the better of her.

"I'll stay with you," Mitchell offered with a big fake grin.

Jessica shuddered and threw herself into Lucas' arms again, the blanket long discarded. "Please, Lucas, do the right thing."

"Oh..." Lucas stuttered. "Okay, fine. Let's find you some spare clothes first, though."

"Oh, you're so chivalrous!" Jessica said cheerily.

Lucas put his arm around the nude redhead and quickly guided her out of the room without meeting Sarah's fiery gaze.

Mitchell sighed and dragged Jack's dead body out of the room without a single ounce of respect.

Sarah looked around at the room. She wasn't sure if it was her jealousy or not, but something didn't seem right.

"You okay?" Komo asked worriedly. "Mind if I take the other bed in the kids' room?"

"Sure," Sarah replied, "and yeah, don't worry. I'm fine," she lied.

DAY 6

Sarah dreamt of darkness and only darkness, nothing but an endless plane of blackness. It felt like she had wandered there for a lifetime, seemingly walking on air in the cold dark emptiness. Many times she tried to call out but no noise left her mouth, and every step she took was silent. Sarah carried on wandering aimlessly, unsure of what to do, in the vain hope that she would find something other than the void.

Her spirits were lifted when a light appeared beneath her. Sarah strained her eyes to see what it was, and suddenly she was hurtling downwards towards the illumination. She came to a stop sharply several yards above a roofless house. Twelve people were wandering about inside. Some sat and cried, and others were hammering on walls and smashing things into the windows and doorways. It looked similar to the House of Twelve but the layout was definitely different, although she couldn't make out the people inside to be sure. Another roofless house flashed into existence beside the first, then another, and then another, until the space beneath her was filled with house after house, each of which had people trapped within.

Sarah tried calling out again but no sound whatsoever passed from her lips. She tried clapping her hands so hard that they stung but even that didn't breach the indomitable silence. A blonde woman in the house below stopped in her tracks, as did others in the distant houses, and Sarah could just about make out one similar looking woman in each house standing idle. In unison, they turned their heads to the sky and Sarah looked down at countless versions of herself.

Sarah awoke in the darkness, but thankfully not the void that she had dreamt of. Light from the hallways seeped in through the cracks of the children's room door, giving her just enough illumination to reach the light switch unhindered. When the light came on she looked hopefully towards the blue bed, but it was unoccupied. The thought of Lucas sleeping beside Jessica in the spare bed made her feel ill.

Melanie was in her element in the master bedroom, cleaning to her heart's content between violent sobbing fits. Sarah looked harshly at the older woman as she walked by, and a nasty thought sprung to mind that made her chuckle: come tomorrow, they'd have to find a new cleaner. Although she couldn't deny the faint hope that Jessica would wind up dead.

When she got to the bathroom and met her own gaze in the mirror, she stared herself in the eyes like she had done on the previous day. The callous and violent thoughts were becoming so natural to her. It was only after they had passed that she questioned them, and that worried her almost more than being trapped inside the House of Twelve. "What's happening to me?" she sighed to herself.

In a split-second flash, her reflection smashed its fists against the mirror and screamed madly at her. Just as Sarah had flinched backwards the reflection had returned to normal, and Sarah stared at it for a while, scared and curious if her reflection would change again.

Sarah's head twitched nervously as she was left wondering if she had imagined the whole thing or not. She quickly left the bathroom and went downstairs to the kitchen.

Lucas was making some food for himself and Jessica, and he looked sheepishly at Sarah when she walked in. "Morning, Sarah," he said, trying to keep his voice from shaking.

"Morning," Sarah replied blankly.

"Lucas is such a gentleman," Jessica said proudly. "He comforted me all night," she added slyly.

"Isn't that nice of him?" Sarah said with a fake grin. She took some water and bread, and made an early start at the window.

"Morning," Komo said wearily. "I couldn't sleep much so I gave up and came down here. Haven't managed much of anything, though," she said, gesturing to the battered brickwork.

"Let's get a move on," Sarah said emotionlessly. She took the sledgehammer and began striking the bricks as hard as she could, forcing herself to focus solely on escaping.

"He's not into her. You know that, right?" Komo said after half an hour or so in awkward silence. "He's just trying to be a gentleman."

Sarah nodded. She was sure Komo was right, but it didn't make her feel any better.

Eventually Mitchell, Jessica, and Lucas joined them at the wall. Jessica spent most of the day flirting with Lucas, and when it was her turn by the window she got him to teach her the best way to use the sledgehammer, giggling playfully throughout. No one mentioned the slightly paranormal events of the day before; as they couldn't explain it, they chose to ignore and forget it. The Wreck and Melanie stayed as far away from each other as possible, and Melanie seemed to avoid being around everyone in general, sensing the animosity towards her.

"I think we'll be through this brickwork in a few days," Mitchell said hopefully. "Then I'm going to find out who put us in here and start taking this hammer to them."

"I'm just going to get as far away from this fucking place as possible," Komo said.

"Same here," Lucas said. "I think we should all tell the police as soon as possible and bring whoever's behind this to justice."

"So noble," Jessica sighed.

"Police?" Mitchell scoffed. "That will go down a treat," he said sarcastically. "Hello, police? We've been trapped in a house for a few days – oh, and we may have killed some people, but we were forced to…"

"They won't punish us," Komo said, but quickly doubted herself. "Will they?"

"Of course not," Lucas said. "We're the victims in this," he added, but his voice trembled slightly.

"Accessories to murder," Mitchell said fatally. "That's what every single survivor of this place is going to be judged as. Trust me, you can't trust the cops. They'll just go for an easy conviction, mark my words."

Sarah's heart was thumping in her chest when she spoke. "I'm with Mitchell," she said fiercely. "Whoever did this has to pay for it. Really pay for it, not just sit behind bars for a bit."

"Sarah, this is getting out of hand," Lucas said disappointedly. "We've got to draw the line somewhere. As soon as we're out of here, we don't have to kill anymore!"

"I don't care," Sarah said coldly. "We've been made to suffer and soon it will be their turn."

Mitchell laughed. "I'm glad at least one of you is seeing sense."

Jessica's eyes glazed over slightly. "I agree. I'm not going down for killing that rapist piece of shit, and I'll feel better knowing that whoever's behind this is rotting in the ground." She blinked a lot and regained her chirpiness. "Sorry Lucas, honey, I just don't think talking to the cops is a good idea at all."

Lucas looked sullen and defeated, and didn't say anything for a long time, even in the face of Jessica's flagrant advances. When he finally did speak, his voice was dry and quiet. "What if it's not that simple?"

"Sorry?" Komo asked.

"You saw the television," Lucas began, "and all that water coming out of the locket."

"It wasn't that much," Mitchell growled dismissively.

"It was more than a little locket should have held," Lucas countered.

"It was very, very weird," Komo said. "But it might just be a side effect of whatever they drugged us with."

"It wouldn't explain why we all saw the same thing," Lucas replied. "People don't have the exact same hallucinations."

"We don't know what they've drugged us with," Sarah said to be awkward.

"Just forget it," Mitchell ordered. "Let's just get out of this fucking house before we all end up dead."

The Wreck shuffled into the room. He hesitantly approached Sarah and handed her a photograph. "I think this is for you," he said, and then he wandered off murmuring to himself.

Sarah looked down at the photo and saw it was the exact one from her dream the other night, the one with a younger version of herself and Darren. It even had the knife mark where she had stabbed the knife through Darren's face.

"How...?" Sarah muttered.

"What is it?" Lucas asked.

"Just me when I was younger. It's nothing," she lied.

Sarah scrunched up the picture and dumped it in the fireplace. She took the opportunity to light the fire, and looked on in satisfaction as the flames obliterated the damn thing. Sarah decided to confront the Wreck about where he had found the photo from her dream. She hunted around the ground floor quickly, and finally she found him hiding under the pool table.

"Where did you get that picture?" she asked as calmly as possible, lowering herself onto the ground so that they were face-to-face.

His worried little eyes darted about until they finally locked onto hers. "It was under your pillow, under the pillow, sometimes the houses leave things about, things to help remember."

"*Houses*? You mean house, right?" Sarah corrected him.

The Wreck nodded. "Okay, house," he muttered unhelpfully.

"He knows more than he's letting on," Melanie said evilly.

Sarah jolted upright in surprise and stood up quickly. "What are you on about?"

"If you listen to what he mutters, there are little snippets of truth in all the babbling," Melanie explained. "I know you're all turning against me, I'm not stupid, but I'm telling you; it's the Wreck you should be worried about. I bet he's the reason we're here." With that, she stormed off out into the hallway.

"Do you know what's going on here?" Sarah asked the Wreck.

"We're all dead, we're all dead," he began sobbing to himself.

Sarah shook her head and went to walk away, but saw Komo by the door.

"Can I have a word?" Komo asked.

"Yeah, of course," Sarah said, wondering what she had to say.

"It's about Lucas and Jessica," Komo began. "I didn't want to say anything before because I didn't want to worry you..."

Sarah's heart sunk, assuming Komo was going to tell her that the two of them had been intimate.

"Oh, it's not that!" Komo said, guessing what Sarah was thinking. "But it is worse, I'm afraid. I'm worried about Lucas."

"What about him?" Sarah said flatly, although truthfully she was relieved that she'd gotten the wrong end of the stick.

"Well, I'm concerned about Jessica's interest in him," Komo hedged. "I don't think she's right – you know, in the head."

"You've only just figured that out?" Sarah chuckled, and then the thought of her own reflection smashing its fists against the mirror popped into her head. After suppressing the urge to shiver, she pushed the thought as far away as possible.

"I don't just mean ditzy," Komo elaborated. "I mean full blown whack-job crazy. She spoke to me one time after Jack had been hitting on me like a creep, and she wasn't herself at all. She was distant and cold, and seemed to have some issue with men."

Sarah remembered her similar run-in with Jessica and nodded in agreement. "I had a similar chat with her. Her eyes were glazed over and she definitely had some sort of grudge, I thought it was just a one-off."

"I've seen it in her eyes," Komo continued. "It's like she's got a split personality or something."

Sarah thought about her recent concerns for her own mind-set but didn't say anything.

"Like I said," Komo carried on, "I didn't want to say anything, but the more I think about last night, the more I question it."

"You don't think Jack was trying to rape her?" Sarah had to agree that something didn't seem quite right about the incident.

"Don't get me wrong, he was definitely a creep, but he'd never hurt Jessica before that night," Komo said. "He might have been a rapist but surely he'd have known that we'd all turn on him if it came out, so why would he try raping her in the hour that someone has to die?"

Sarah gave it some thought. "Well, he was probably going to kill her shortly after so that would have saved his skin, and the rest of us, for the night."

"But then we would've killed him tonight for raping Jessica," Komo challenged.

"Yeah... good point," Sarah agreed.

"And the way she was all over Lucas after someone had just tried assaulting her," Komo continued, "the whole thing doesn't add up."

"We should warn Lucas," Sarah said, trying to hide just how pleased she was at having an excuse to drive a wedge between Jessica and Lucas.

"No," Komo said quickly. "He'll only think we're being jealous or something, and she'll probably play on that. We should keep an eye out and watch for anything concrete we can confront her with."

"Or we could get her tonight," Sarah said plainly.

"Excuse me?" Komo asked, surprised.

"Let's cut to the chase; she's bad and we know it," Sarah said harshly. "So tonight when everyone's going for Melanie – who seems to know what we will do, by the way – Jessica will have a *little accident* first."

"I'm sorry, I thought I was talking to Sarah, not Mitchell," Komo said chidingly.

Sarah scowled. "So what was your plan, huh? Find out she's a psycho and just sit on your ass and hope someone else deals with her? Or pray that she randomly drops dead between eleven and midnight?"

Komo flinched backwards from the surprising verbal assault. "I just didn't think you were like *that*."

Sarah rubbed her eyes. Her head was starting to hurt badly. "I'm sorry, Komo. This place is really starting to get to me, and it just doesn't help seeing Jessica all over Darren like that. I know now isn't the time for that kind of thing, but I *like* him."

"Who's Darren?" Komo asked.

"Lucas. Sorry, I meant Lucas!" Sarah couldn't believe she'd let that slip.

"I figured that. I still want to know who Darren is," Komo pressed.

Sarah hesitated. "Just someone I used to know."

"Is he the person out of that picture the Wreck gave you?"

"Yeah, just an old flame. Bit of a sore subject... so, have you figured out anything about the picture you found?" Sarah said, trying to change the subject.

"No," Komo said sadly. "Sometimes I think I've got it, but my head hurts the more I think about it."

"Can't we remember?" the Wreck said, getting out from under the pool table and shuffling off. "Or is it that we don't want to remember?"

Komo and Sarah returned to the living room window and reflected thoughtfully on the Wreck's cryptic words. Sarah started to wonder if Melanie was actually right about him.

The group did what they could at the window and ate lightly in-between, finally coming to a stop at what the clock was showing as half ten at night. They were all becoming far more fatigued as each day went by. The lack of good food, the restless nights or complete lack of sleep entirely, and the days of hammering at an unnaturally strong bricked-up window frame was visibly taking its toll. The only thing that kept them going was the knowledge that soon they would break through.

Sarah, Jessica, Lucas, Komo, and Mitchell gathered in the parlour. They decided against talking in the kitchen in case Melanie wandered in for a late-night snack.

"So when that weird music stops, I'll kill Melanie," Mitchell said casually.

The group sullenly agreed, except for Lucas who seemed thoughtful. "We only tried doing nothing for one night," he said sadly.

"We almost all died for that," Mitchell grumbled, angry that Lucas was dragging out the verdict.

"But we don't know that for sure. I mean, what if it was a one-off just to scare us into killing?" Lucas argued.

"I'm not risking it, end of discussion," Mitchell growled.

"Who put you in charge?" Jessica asked angrily. "Lucas is smart, maybe he's right?"

"Melanie's not the nicest of people," Komo said, "but I'd rather not kill her if there was another way. Would waiting to see if the gas comes out again be that much of an issue?"

"She spoke to me earlier," Sarah said. "She knows what we're planning. If we wait, it gives her more time to prepare."

"I don't know why we're still debating this," Mitchell growled. "It's going to happen."

The group argued amongst themselves until the music stopped, and the overwhelming silence swept through the house. They were just about to start talking again when they heard a whining from upstairs. They strained their ears to try and figure out what it was, but it soon stopped. Just as they were about to ask each other what it could've been, they heard a quick cry and thumping on the floorboards.

"Melanie's going to kill the Wreck," Sarah gasped. The older woman had been preparing, but not to defend herself. She knew if she killed the Wreck before the group killed her then she would be safe for another day.

"The fuck she is!" Mitchell roared, and he stormed into the hallway and up the stairs.

Everyone else followed hot on his trail, but by the time they got up the stairs he was already shoulder-barging the bathroom door.

"Mitchell, I can pick that!" Komo said frantically.

"No time," Mitchell grunted, shoving all of his weight and strength into another strike. "It sounds like... she's drowning him!"

Mitchell once again smashed into the wooden door and successfully busted it open. He toppled into the bathroom to see Melanie forcing the Wreck under the water. The poor man was struggling and splashing in a losing battle to get the woman off him and gulp down what air he could every time he managed to get his mouth above the surface.

Melanie glanced at Mitchell, who was regaining his footing as quickly as possible, and pushed the Wreck down under the slightly discoloured water in a last ditch attempt to drown him before the others killed her. She risked another sideward glance but felt a hand on the back of her head. She squealed as the hand tugged her head back by the hair, and then everything went black as her head hurtled towards the edge of the bathtub.

Mitchell grabbed the Wreck up in his arms like a baby, carried him out onto the landing, and sat him up against the wall. The poor Wreck spat up a mouthful of water, gasping and wheezing as he hungrily swallowed as much air as he could.

"The music's still not playing," Sarah said coldly.

"She isn't dead yet," Mitchell said getting to his feet. "Look after him," he growled to the group.

"Do it fast," Lucas said regretfully. "She doesn't need to suffer."

Mitchell smiled evilly as he looked back at the group. "Oh, yes she does," he said, and he closed the busted bathroom door behind him.

DAY 7

Screams and gargling noises came from behind the bathroom door shortly after Mitchell had closed it. Jessica went into the spare bedroom, dragging Lucas along with her, so Sarah went to carry on working at the window.

"You need rest," Komo said following her. "It won't be any good to us if you're too exhausted to help tomorrow."

The music came back on but Sarah and Komo barely noticed.

Sarah was grateful that Komo was concerned, but another part of her just wanted to tell her to piss off. "I won't be up too late," Sarah promised. "I'll sleep soon, but I just need to tire myself out first."

"Okay, well make sure that you do," Komo said with a smile. "We might just be able to get out of here without another death if we really go for it tomorrow."

Komo left the living room at just the right moment to see Melanie's limp body hurtling down the stairs. Her head was soaking wet, and her lifeless bloodshot eyes locked with Komo's when she came to a stop by the base of the stairs. Komo yelped in shock. She had hated Melanie, but it was another thing entirely to see her dead.

Mitchell plodded down the stairs cheerfully and grabbed Melanie by her dripping wet hair, pulling her along towards the kitchen without a care in the world.

"We'd better hope we do, or that could be us next," Sarah said grimly in Komo's ear before returning to the brickwork again. She imagined Jessica and her sister's face on the crumbling, cracking bricks every time she struck them with the hammer.

Sarah worked longer than she should've done, but still retreated upstairs before it got ridiculously late. The smell of burning flesh oozing up from the basement certainly helped to drive her away from her sledgehammer overtime.

Sleep came easy for her but it was far from restful, and her nightmare made her wish she'd stayed at the living room window all night. Sarah awoke covered in cold sweat and was shaking all over. Her head rang with pain, her stomach burned and churned, and her throat felt as if she had been violently sick. For the first time since she'd slept in the House of Twelve, she'd had extreme difficulty in remembering most of her dream, and struggling to grasp the details caused the same awful headaches that trying to remember her past did.

All that she could remember from the dream was that she had been in her car, an exquisite white sports car; a benefit of a life bereft of children and commitments. Sarah had been driving fast, too fast to be legal, but that didn't worry her. Nor did the bloody knife on the passenger's seat. She was going to pay someone a visit, a fatal one, just like the visit she had made earlier. The night's sky was a void of pure darkness, and every house that her car whizzed past had bricked-up windows and doors.

Sarah pulled herself out of the bed with a great deal of effort. There was more to the dream but she couldn't force herself to remember, and what she did know worried her too much to focus on.

Sarah considered the Wreck's words once again. Maybe she really didn't want to remember.

She stumbled slowly towards the bathroom, forgetting for the moment what had happened there the night before, and began to run a warm bath to wash away her clamminess. Sarah watched as the discoloured water filled the tub, and only then did she snap out of her sleepy reverie.

There was dried blood on the side of the bathtub. The door was barely on its hinges, there was cracked plaster and black shoe marks on the walls where Melanie had struggled, and clumps of long hair were discarded on the floor. Sarah looked at the murder scene with her weary eyes and knew that she should care, but chose not to. She undressed and got into the bathtub, sinking underneath the warm water and emptying her head of any and all troublesome thoughts. When she arose, Sarah took a deep breath and wiped the water from her eyes. She tasted a coppery metallic tang in her mouth, and when she looked around she was in an endless sea of bubbling blood under a black sky. Her head twitched, and she was back in the bathtub staring stupidly at the bathroom walls. Sarah climbed out and got dry as quickly as she could, afraid to be alone in the room any longer, and then got dressed. The whole time, she avoided glancing in the mirror just in case her reflection took on a life of its own again.

"I need out of this fucking house," Sarah mumbled angrily to herself before going downstairs.

The others were already waiting for her in the kitchen. They had made some toast and were discussing their dreams and broken memories.

"I think I shot him, but it wasn't on purpose!" Komo was saying, looking at the picture of the security guard and his apparent family.

"It's a bit hard to shoot someone accidently," Mitchell chuckled. "Especially if they're chasing you down and planning to put a stop to your 'perfect heist'."

"Okay, I meant to shoot him," Komo corrected. "But I didn't mean to kill him. I was aiming for his leg."

"And you got lucky and got him in the chest," Mitchell said, bored. "You told us that already."

"I didn't get *lucky!*" Komo said defensively. "I didn't want him to die. Oh god, why couldn't he have just gone after the others?"

Sarah grabbed some food and drink, and added to the conversation. "You don't know for sure that any of that happened."

"I'm pretty sure, Sarah," Komo said regretfully.

"Worry about it when we're free," Sarah said sternly. "There's no way to tell what's real and what's not in this place anymore."

"Sarah's right," Lucas said. "We have no way of knowing what happened before we woke up here. They could have brainwashed us or hypnotised us—"

"I killed people," Mitchell interrupted casually. "Good people, bad people, people who owed me money..."

"Somehow that doesn't surprise me," Jessica said dryly, before rapidly blinking her eyes and going silly again. "You're such a fierce man, after all. You've got that whole lumberjack thing going for you."

"It was just a way of life to me," Mitchell carried on as if the girl hadn't spoken. "I had my reasons. I can't remember what but I'm pretty sure about it, and I can deal with being a bad person. What bothers me is trying to figure out what happened to my brother, and I just can't get my head around it. When I try, I get the worst fucking headaches ever."

"Seriously, don't focus on it," Sarah reiterated. "Not unless you want a migraine from hell."

"Sounds like you're talking from experience," Mitchell said with a raised eyebrow.

"I am, and all I have to show for it is no answers and a sore fucking head," Sarah lied. She wanted out of the house as soon as possible, and sitting around debating pointless shards of memories wasn't going to help.

"You're right," Mitchell said, getting up and taking the bait. "No point going over this crap while we're captives. Let's get out of here."

Everyone got up and went to the living room. It was obvious that people were wondering who was going to die that night, but no one wanted to raise it first. The general unspoken collective hope was that they would be free well in advance of midnight, and throughout the day they truly gave it their all, barely stopping to rest. All the while the Wreck sat by the fireplace, scribbling in the back of books and then throwing them straight into the fire. It looked like he was trying to teach himself how to write, but as he was causing no harm to anyone the group carried on as they were and left him to it.

One by one, members of the group began to tire. They had strained themselves and expended too much of their energy early on, and by the early evening they could barely make an impact. The clock was pointing to eighteen when they finally decided to give themselves a break.

Sarah caught Komo when she was all alone. "It looks like someone will have to go, after all."

"I know what you're going to say and you can forget it," Komo said, entirely unimpressed.

"You know she's a threat, though!" Sarah argued.

"I know that she's a potential threat to Lucas," Komo retorted, "who seems perfectly okay, by the way. To date, she's killed one rapist. Personally, I think she's more of a threat to you and your insanely ill-timed crush, to be honest."

Sarah grabbed Komo by the arm and spoke severely. "Whatever the reason, you know that if one of us dies then it should be her. You warned me about her!"

Komo looked conflicted. She liked Sarah and could see that Jessica wasn't quite right in the head, but the longer the ordeal in the house went on, the more she could see that Sarah wasn't quite right either. Then there was the overwhelming guilt from the shooting that Komo thought she'd committed. Maybe she was just as crazy when it came down to it. "I... don't want to be a killer," Komo stuttered sadly.

"You don't have to be," Sarah said reassuringly. "Everyone will probably want to draw lots like we discussed the other night. All I need you to do is fiddle it a little bit. Use some of those thief wiles and some sleight of hand."

"You really don't sound like you know what you're talking about," Komo interrupted with half a smile.

Sarah looked pleadingly into Komo's eyes. "Just make sure her name comes up, however we all decide on picking, and then Mitchell will do the rest. She's bad, Komo. I know it sounds jealous and I know it sounds crazy, but I just *know* that she's better off out of the way!"

"I don't like it," Komo said defeated, "but I'd rather have you and Lucas about than her. Not so fussed about Mitchell, to be honest. He's quite threatening, but I'd rather not leave it to chance and lose you two."

"It will save you, too," Sarah reminded her.

Komo looked shocked. "Yeah, I suppose it will." She genuinely hadn't thought about that.

"You're too good for this place, Komo," Sarah said with a big smile. "And thank you. You won't regret this, I promise."

"Make sure that I don't," Komo said gravely, hoping that the path she was on was in fact the right one.

Suddenly, a thought popped into Komo's head. No one had inspected the weird twenty-four hour numbered clock, and so she went to investigate. A flutter of hope rose in her heart. If they were lucky, very lucky, then the gas was being controlled by the clock, so if she tampered with it or switched it off completely then they could buy themselves some time. No doubt whoever put them in the House of Twelve would have a contingency plan in place, but they only needed a little bit more time to get through the window. If Komo could buy them any more time, even if it was a few hours, then it may save someone's life.

Komo went into the living room taking a screwdriver with her, and began carefully inspecting the old clock.

"Nothing in there, nothing out there, nothing in there, nothing out there," the Wreck hummed, still practising his writing while Komo worked.

She couldn't figure out if his words were directed at her or not, but she responded anyway. "We'll see... we'll see."

Komo managed to flick the back of the clock open to reveal the clockwork or digital mechanisms within, but instead, it was just a hollow copper-coloured cylinder with half a dozen glossy square bits of paper inside. Komo stared at the empty space in shock before slowly pulling the bits of paper out. They were small photos from a photo booth, just the right size for a passport or driver's licence, and they were all of Jessica beside various men. Scribbled on the back of each one was a love heart around a different male name and a different female name, but they were all unmistakably of Jessica.

"Nothing in there, nothing out there, nothing in there, nothing out there," the Wreck continued.

"How... how do you know?" Komo asked pleadingly.

"You're not the first to try, you're not the last, you might even try again," the Wreck answered unhelpfully.

Komo looked at the Wreck and wondered just how much information was locked inside his scrambled mind. He was the only member of the group who may know the reasons behind their captivity and a potential way out, and he wasn't able to communicate properly. Komo sighed at the irony.

She put the clock back the way it was, hoping that the mechanism that worked it was somehow hidden and had slipped her attention, and looked closer at the pictures of Jessica. The men all looked happy, ecstatically so, but there was something sinister in Jessica's eyes. Komo was about to take them to Jessica and tell the others about the clock, when she decided against it. Things were getting messed up enough as it was without her making them worse. She put the little photos on the fire and made sure they were reduced to ashes.

"Some things are better off not mentioned," Komo said quietly to the Wreck.

The Wreck nodded and carried on with whatever it was he was trying to achieve with his pen and paper scribbles.

After the group was feeling a little bit more rested they tried to breach the brickwork again, but as they all silently knew, their efforts to escape that night were not going to be successful. Just as Sarah had predicted earlier in the day, the group gathered to discuss making a fair choice at quarter to eleven at night in the kitchen, except for Jessica who wanted to get clean after a hard day of toiling.

"We just couldn't do it," Lucas said tiredly.

"I can't believe how fucking close we are!" Mitchell groaned. He was aching all over.

"If we don't rest, it just lessens the chances of escape tomorrow," Sarah said remorsefully, "and if we run into our captors then we're going to need all of the strength and stamina we have."

"But that means one of us has to die," Lucas said sadly.

"I don't suppose there are any volunteers?" Mitchell chuckled sarcastically.

"How should we decide?" Sarah asked, trying to avoid making eye contact with Komo. "Draw lots like we suggested the other night?"

Komo thought about the pictures she'd found in the clock and decided to commit herself to Sarah's plan. "Sounds fair to me. We put the names in a bowl and get someone to pick one out."

"But who?" Sarah asked, almost like she was reading off a script.

"The Wreck," Komo said firmly. "We just ask him to pluck one out. His name won't be in there and he's the only one who's not biased. I don't think he has the capacity to be on anyone's side, even if he could see whose name was on there."

"Sounds okay to me," Sarah said with an appreciative nod.

"That's fine with me, I don't think there's any other way," Lucas said grimly. "But we should wait until the last minute like we were going to do yesterday, just in case the gas threat was a one-off."

"It's settled, then," Mitchell said, rubbing his hands together. "I don't think my name should be put in, though."

"What? Why not?" Lucas asked, shocked.

"I'm the strongest here," Mitchell said with a shrug. "Good luck getting out of here without me."

"You can't expect us to go along with that!" Lucas said flabbergasted. "You know we'll still get through without you."

"How long will it take you, though?" Mitchell asked with a sly smile. "Another night? Two, maybe?"

Lucas went to speak but Sarah cut him off. "He's right, Lucas. It's shitty and unfair but he's right."

"How can you be okay with that?" Lucas asked in confusion.

"I don't like it," Komo said, trying to sound convincing, "but Mitchell is right. We risk losing more without him."

"Good, glad you all see sense," Mitchell said cheerfully.

Lucas looked around as if he was the only sane one in the room, and then finally conceded defeat. "Okay, fine. Only Jessica, Sarah, Komo and my own name will go in, and the Wreck will pull one out."

Everyone nodded, and once again Lucas looked around longingly, hoping that some other fair solution would manifest itself, but the others just stayed silent.

"I'll go and tell Jessica," Lucas said sadly before leaving the room.

He made his way upstairs as Jessica was just walking down, and she was wearing nothing but a bath towel wrapped around her body.

"Oh good, Lucas, I need to show you something!" she said urgently.

"What is it? We need to talk about tonight," he replied.

"That can wait; I think I've found a way out!" she said, dragging him by the arm.

Without saying another word she led him into the master bedroom and pointed at its bricked-up window, just as the background music fell silent.

"There," she said, pointing at the bricks. "They're loose!"

Lucas walked over to the window and inspected them thoroughly. "Are you sure? They look fine to me."

"Is that the only thing in the room that looks *fine?*" Jessica asked smoothly.

Lucas turned around to see that Jessica had dropped the towel to the floor. She was stretching seductively, emphasising her body's fine curves.

"Jessica!" Lucas said, turning away in embarrassment. "Please, we can't..."

"You're a very noble man, Lucas Adams," she said admiringly. "But still a man, nonetheless," Jessica added in a strange tone. "I was serious about the window. Look closer."

Blushing heavily, Lucas gave the window a closer look. He traced the cement with his finger, searching for what Jessica was trying to point out to him.

"Lucas, look out!" Sarah cried from the doorway. She had come to check on him, and rightly so; Jessica was looming over him with a sharp knife.

Lucas caught her arms in his hands, but the crazed woman brought the knife closer and closer to his chest. Lucas tried to angle the knife away from him but Jessica was forcing it towards him with all of her weight and strength.

Sarah looked around wildly for a weapon, but Melanie had done too much of a good job in tidying the room. There was no viable option but to join the struggle herself. She rushed over and wrenched the woman's arms back, and combined with Lucas pushing her away, Jessica tumbled backwards on top of Sarah. Sarah's head knocked into the floor causing her to see sparks, but the anger was rising from her chest again. She was going to kill the bitch if it was the last thing she did. She scrambled back onto her feet but Jessica was already lunging at Lucas. This time he was ready though, and with a groan he embraced the naked woman. Sarah looked on fearfully, expecting Lucas to fall down dead, but instead Jessica dropped to her knees. Lucas had reversed the attack, twisting the knife back on his attacker and using her own force to press it into her chest.

Jessica spat blood at him. "You filthy, lying, cheating man," she hissed demonically as she pulled the knife from her bare chest.

Sarah smacked her in the back of the head as hard as she could, fearing that she would attack again, and Jessica fell face down onto the floor. Lucas looked on in shock and horror, staring at the blood on his hands in a fear-stricken trance. Jessica tried to pick herself off the floor but Sarah kicked and stamped at the pretty woman's head, over and over, until the music began playing once again.

DAY 8

Sarah slept like a baby that night, and no nightmares or cryptic dreams haunted her peaceful slumber.

The group had rushed upstairs shortly after the music had turned back on to see what the commotion was, although they all had known it was going to involve someone's death. Sarah had explained what had happened on Lucas' behalf, as he had been deep in shock.

"So much for drawing lots," Mitchell had said. "I guess we're the survivors, then."

Sarah had given Komo an '*I told you so*' look and she had grimaced in reply.

Mitchell had taken the fresh duvet from the bed and wrapped Jessica's bleeding corpse in it before carting it down to the basement, and Sarah had guided Lucas to the bathroom to help clean himself up before settling him down like a child in the blue bed. The whole time, Sarah had tried her best to contain her elation. If anything, things had gone even better than how she'd planned them. Lucas was hers once more.

Sarah awoke feeling fresh, eager, and ready to smash the bricked-up living room window into smithereens. Lucas was sitting up on his bed; he looked very tired and had definitely had a rough night.

"Are you okay?" Sarah asked sympathetically.

Lucas nodded solemnly. "Thank you for last night, I would've been finished if it wasn't for you."

Sarah went and sat beside him. She took his hand in hers and looked deeply into his eyes. "You don't need to thank me, I was just concerned. I care for you deeply, after all. I knew that Lisa was trouble."

"Lisa?" Lucas asked.

"Did I say that?" Sarah asked, trying to sound surprised. She had done it again, and she was pretty sure that Lisa was her sister's name.

"Yeah, you did," Lucas said, trying not to sound worried.

"Sorry, I must be a bit dozy still. Lisa was a friend of mine," she lied, "or at least, she was. I caught her stealing from me so I told her never to come near me again. On a brighter note I actually had a good night of sleep, no creepy nightmares. What about you?" she pressed, trying to change the subject.

"Lucky you," Lucas said enviously. "I dreamt that I was counting the money in my wallet and before I knew it I was falling down an endless flight of stairs."

"Ouch," Sarah said, pulling a face.

"Tell me about it," Lucas said, trying not to remember the pain.

"On an even better note," Sarah began with a big smile, "we'll be out of this horrible place today!"

Lucas perked up. "We better be ready for what's on the other side, but it will be a relief to escape. Are you still hell-bent on getting revenge?"

Sarah shook her head. "I don't know why I said that, I was just angry. I'm just going to follow you. We'll let Mitchell go on the hunt for our bloody captors," she joked.

Lucas smiled. "I'm glad, the last thing we need is more blood on our hands."

They went downstairs and fixed up some basic breakfast for the survivors as they were the first up. They were soon joined by the other three, and the five captive residents ate quickly. They were all looking forward to achieving their hard-earned escape from the House of Twelve.

After each strike of the hammer, the rest of the group observed enthusiastically, hoping that it would be the one to break through, but it wasn't until the afternoon that they finally pierced the wall.

Mitchell pressed his eye to the small hole that they'd made at the centre of the dusty crumbling crater and strained his sight as much as he could. "I can't see anything," he said worriedly.

"The clock might be wrong," Komo said, remembering that it was in fact empty of inner workings. "It could actually be night out there."

"Go arm yourselves," Mitchell commanded, as he prepared to widen the weak spot their hard endeavours had finally produced.

"Good thinking," Lucas said. "We'd best get ready for a fight."

Sarah, Lucas and Komo went to the kitchen and picked out the meanest looking knives they could find. They considered looking in the basement for something more 'heavy duty', but none of them wanted to go down to Mitchell's makeshift crematorium.

Mitchell grunted and groaned as he slammed the sledgehammer into the crumbling brickwork, sending splinters and shards of the extremely durable bricks out into the darkness outside, and with a sigh of relief the surrounding bricks finally began to break away. They separated at their cemented seams just like they were supposed to. The others re-joined him just in time to see the window open up wholly, and they looked through the gap in dumbfounded disbelief. There was nothing beyond; just pure black nothingness.

Sarah instantly thought of her nightmares. "No," she uttered.

"It's not possible!" Mitchell roared. He picked up a loose brick and threw it outside, but they never heard it hit the floor. It was just gone.

Komo stared out into the endless void in total disbelief.

"We should find a torch," Lucas said frantically. "Maybe there's something out there that we can't see."

"Yeah," Sarah muttered, "Yeah, let's look. Come on, Komo."

"Nothing in there, nothing out there..." Komo said, imitating what the Wreck had said.

"Nothing out there, nothing out there," the Wreck sobbed, scurrying away as quickly as he could.

The captives scurried around the house in a frantic effort to find a torch. They were so eager to leave, and even more eager to deny what they knew in their hearts to be true. Mitchell found one in the basement, regrouped with Lucas, Sarah, and Komo, and rushed back to the living room. The torch fell from his hand when he looked upon the window, and the others whimpered in disbelief. The window was bricked-up again.

"No, no, no!" Mitchell screamed. He picked up the hammer and began smashing it into the fully restored brickwork, and it didn't budge an inch. His attacks didn't even leave a mark this time.

Komo hurried off, crying to herself. Sarah went to follow but Lucas put his hand on her shoulder and shook his head. "Give her some space."

"What are we going to do?" Sarah asked, afraid.

"I don't know," Lucas admitted.

"You know what this means," Mitchell said, staring at the bricks. "Only one of us is going to make it out of here alive. I suppose that's the rule of this game."

"The rules," Lucas gasped. "Maybe we missed something!"

Sarah nodded doubtfully. The horrifying realisation that they were dealing with a very paranormal situation was overpowering her hopeful denial.

Lucas read the rules out loud again. "Redemption is the key to escape," he repeated thoughtfully a few times.

"How do we 'redeem' ourselves?" Sarah asked dryly.

"We don't," Mitchell said angrily. "It's just written there to mess with our heads. Whatever has us here wants bloodshed. That's all there is to it."

"I think there's more to it than that, there just has to be," Lucas said confidently.

"If you say so," Mitchell said as he slumped down on the sofa in front of the broken television, and he stared at it without blinking.

Sarah and Lucas looked at each other with concern. They both knew just how dire the situation was, and being locked in a house with Mitchell the survivalist wouldn't end well for either of them.

"We're going to find Komo," Sarah said, gesturing for Lucas to follow.

"Yeah, we'll see you soon," Lucas said leaving the living room.

Mitchell made no attempt to engage with either of them, and just continued staring into space.

"If we can't figure this shit out then we are totally fucked," Sarah whispered to Lucas in hushed tones. She had led him into the parlour, beside the pool table.

"I know, I know," he said frantically. "What do you think *this* is?" he asked, gesturing to the walls surrounding them.

"Nightmare, hell, ghosts, aliens, magic, computer simulation..." Sarah listed half-heartedly. "Fuck knows."

"How is redemption going to free us?" Lucas moaned. "And how do we achieve it?"

"Don't stress over it, the house is just messing with us," Sarah said miserably. "We should be more worried about surviving Mitchell."

"All the things we've found though–" Lucas began.

"Clues to help us remember," the Wreck interrupted from beneath the pool table. "If we want to."

Sarah and Lucas both jumped, but Lucas quickly recovered from the shock and knelt down to talk with the Wreck.

"Who are you, really?" Lucas asked curiously. "What do you know about this place, and do you know a way out?"

"I'm... working on it," the Wreck said, scribbling on the inside of a book.

"Working on what?" Lucas asked in confusion.

"All of it," the Wreck said confidently before returning to his scribbles.

"Come on," Sarah said, putting her hand on Lucas' shoulder. "Let's go and find Komo."

Lucas got up reluctantly but carried on looking at the Wreck, wondering if the right combination of words would unlock the secrets within his scrambled brain.

"Maybe Komo's working on a plan, or maybe between the three of us we can work out how to live a bit longer," Sarah said, drawing Lucas away.

They searched around the house for Komo starting with the kitchen, then each bedroom, and then the bathroom, and finally – reluctantly – they called and peeked down the stairs into the gore-stricken basement. She was nowhere to be found.

They went back to the living room and asked Mitchell if he'd seen her. He was still sitting down watching something on the television.

"Mitchell, has Komo been in here?" Sarah asked.

Mitchell shook his head and carried on watching the television. Something was playing on repeat.

"Sarah," Lucas said, nudging her with his elbow. "The television."

"Yeah, what about it...?" she began to ask, but remembered with a surge of spine-chilling terror that it had been broken the last time they saw it.

"It fixed itself," Lucas gasped.

"That's impossible... just like the window. Maybe this is all a bad dream," Sarah stuttered.

"If only we knew how to wake up," Lucas said numbly.

Sarah walked towards the television with Lucas following behind, and looked at what Mitchell was viewing. There was a man on the screen, a rough and tough looking brute in a dusty suit, and behind him was a young man hanging by his feet from a warehouse ceiling.

"You hurt us, Mitchell, so now we're going to hurt you," the television repeated over and over like a broken record.

"That's my brother there," Mitchell growled quietly, "hanging by that chain."

"Let's turn that off," Sarah said, concerned. An angrier Mitchell was the last thing they needed.

She approached the television, and it suddenly changed to two little girls in white dresses. They had long blonde hair and looked like they could be twins. Their eyes were sunken and their skin was deathly white. "Are you sorry, Sarah? Are you sorry?" they asked over and over. Sarah angrily flicked the off switch and luckily the screen went black. She watched it for a moment to make sure it was still off before turning to face the others.

"Who were they?" Lucas asked.

"No one," Sarah said grumpily. She didn't want to talk about Lisa and Darren's daughters. "Mitchell, are you sure that Komo hasn't been in here?"

"I haven't seen her since we saw the... *nothingness* outside," he grumbled back.

"We can't find her anywhere," Lucas said.

Mitchell's eyes went wide like someone had suddenly flicked his 'on switch' or given him a slap across the face. "Have you checked the kitchen?"

"Yeah, she's not in there," Sarah replied.

"I don't mean *her*," Mitchell roared. "I mean the food!"

"She wouldn't..." Lucas stammered.

"We're in here for the long haul and she's no cold-blooded killer," Mitchell said heatedly. "What other options would she really have now?"

"Let's go and check," Sarah said calmly, "but I'm telling you, she isn't like that."

The group went to the kitchen and Sarah's jaw dropped. Mitchell was one hundred percent right; Komo had taken all the food and water.

"Fuck it!" Mitchell shouted. "Where is she?!" He stormed off and stomped around the house.

Sarah and Lucas joined the search, taking on a much friendlier approach than the brutish Mitchell, but they couldn't find her anywhere. Eventually they gave up and sat together miserably at the dining table.

"I can't believe she's left us to starve," Sarah said, upset. "I thought we were friends."

"She's obviously snapped and gone into survival mode," Lucas sighed.

They could hear Mitchell stomping around upstairs, screaming her name.

"We're going to have to be ready for him," Sarah said, gesturing to the ceiling.

"I know," Lucas said gloomily. "We'll stay armed and together at all times. Apart from that, I'm out of ideas."

Sarah nodded. Their situation seemed hopelessly fatal.

They sat and talked for the rest of the day. Their stomachs growled and their mouths were dry, but they were unable to find anything to eat or drink. They considered drinking from the taps but decided to wait until there was no other option left. All the while, Mitchell continued his rage-filled hunt for Komo. When the clock hit twenty-three, Sarah and Lucas waited nervously for Mitchell to come for one of them. Instead, they heard more knocking from upstairs.

"What the fuck is he up to?" Sarah whispered.

"Maybe he's found Komo," Lucas replied quietly.

"Should we go and have a look?" she asked nervously.

"I suppose we could. If he's coming for us then he'll find us, no matter where we are," Lucas said grimly.

They walked slowly up the stairs, making sure that they had at least two knives each that were readily available should the worst come to the worst. They were half way up the stairs when they heard banging and screaming from the ceiling above.

"Fuck!" Sarah gasped. "He's found her!"

They quickly ran up the stairs and saw a rickety fold-down staircase on the landing hallway, leading to a previously hidden attic above. There was a broom discarded on the floor; Mitchell had been poking around for any hidden nooks and crannies, and obviously got lucky. Sarah and Lucas looked at each other in a silent debate whether or not to go up into the attic, but it wasn't long before Mitchell was walking down them with his arms filled with what was left of the food and water supplies.

"No need to thank me," Mitchell said, barging past them.

The music began to play again. It might have been their imaginations, but now it seemed much louder than it had been before.

DAY 9

Sarah had gone into the attic shortly after Mitchell was out of the way. It was almost pitch black except for two dingy flickering light bulbs at each end, but there was very little of worth to illuminate. There were piles of torn cardboard boxes filled with old newspapers and clothing, crates filled with worthless bric-a-brac, and piles of broken toys, decorations, and old furniture. Swinging from a beam in the centre of the room had been Komo, hanging from her neck by a thick rope Mitchell had found amongst the mess. Lucas had helped Sarah to lower her down. Both of them had stood precariously on whatever they could use to reach the beam, and together they laid Komo's body down on the dusty floor and covered it with an old sheet.

"That's not escape either, so what is?" the Wreck had said, after popping his head up through the hatch.

"No more games!" Sarah had yelled. "What aren't you telling us?"

The Wreck had covered his face with his hands defensively and sobbed. "I don't know, I don't know, I can't put the pieces together!" he had cried as he'd run away.

Lucas had stopped Sarah from following. "Let's eat and go to bed. Maybe we'll dream our way free," he'd added sarcastically.

Unfortunately for Sarah, Lucas' sarcastic comment did not come true. Once she had finally drowned out the awful repeating background music, she fell into yet another unpleasant slumber.

She was standing in a beautiful church filled with mingling people dressed in their finest clothes. Sarah looked down at herself and saw that she was wearing an amazingly lavish wedding dress. Her heart skipped a beat, and she realised what was happening. This was her wedding day to Darren.

The talking guests began getting louder, their whispers and mumbled comments combining until their collective voices oozed together and became one endless buzz of droning noise. They were amused, entertained by her anxiety. Some of them had warned her beforehand, but she had ignored them. She knew that they were wrong. But as she waited alone at the altar her heart began to sink, and as the stained-glass windows began to brick themselves up, she was forced to face the facts. Darren wasn't coming. Suddenly the church erupted in roars of laughter, each guest almost keeling over as they pointed and laughed at her pain and anguish. Sarah looked around for a friendly face, just one person to help her through it, but even her own parents were joining in with the rest. The one thing she did notice in her hopeless search for sympathy was the empty space reserved for her sister, Lisa. Anger flooded into her mind, her stomach tingled as the adrenaline rush coursed through her pounding blood vessels, and one by one the guests dropped dead, stabbed to death dozens of times with invisible blades. Sarah felt relieved, and better than she'd felt in a long time. Seeing their stupid dead faces and flowing blood filled her with an immense sense of satisfaction. She didn't care how crazy that made her. The people that had hurt her were gone, and that was all that mattered; well, except for Lisa and Darren. The church began filling with blood, and before

Sarah knew it she was waist deep in the warm bubbling liquid. She didn't bother looking for an exit as she already knew they'd be bricked up or locked, so she allowed the blood to flow over her head and deprive her of air. Her only regret was not killing Darren and Lisa for what they had done.

Sarah woke up gasping for air. It took her a moment to realise that she wasn't actually drowning, and she sat upright and allowed herself a moment to catch her breath before getting out of bed.

Lucas was already up so she went downstairs to find him, and Sarah found him sitting at the dining table looking worried. He had made her some breakfast and poured her a glass of water. She thanked him, and they ate in silence. She didn't want to talk about her nightmare, and from the look in his weary eyes neither did Lucas.

The rest of the day passed by slow and uneventfully. The feeling of entrapment was overwhelming, and knowing that there was no foreseeable way out of the House of Twelve had finally broken what little spirits they had remaining. Mitchell avoided them and they avoided Mitchell. The three of them knew it would end in bloodshed between them, and they didn't bother with false courtesies. The only one who seemed unaffected by the miserable and grave situation was the Wreck, who seemed to have made a breakthrough with his writing and was acting very pleased with himself.

While Lucas and Sarah were sitting together on the sofa trying to force some conversation, the Wreck wandered in and looked up at the ceiling.

"I think I remember," the Wreck said, "but I don't understand. How do I atone for what I've done? How do I redeem myself?"

Lucas and Sarah were speechless. It was the most lucid they'd ever seen the Wreck, even though he was talking to the ceiling. They heard the letterbox clattering and they ran into the hallway. Sarah banged violently on the metal door while Lucas picked up what had been delivered. It was a letter addressed to a Philip Doyle.

The Wreck walked along and took the letter out of Lucas' hands. "That's for me, thanks," he said with a sad smile before going back to the living room.

"So the Wreck is Philip," Lucas said, "and the house answered him."

Sarah stopped pounding the door. "This is getting more and more fucked up."

They went into the living room and saw that Philip had finished reading the letter, and he folded it up and put it into the fire. "Thank you," he said to the ceiling. "I understand now."

Before Sarah and Lucas could ask him what the letter had said, he scurried off and that was the last they saw of him.

"I don't suppose you want to tell us how to escape?!" Sarah shouted at the house.

The television turned on and showed an image of the house rules resting on the coffee table.

"Thanks for nothing," Sarah muttered angrily, and she messed with the switch until it was off again.

"There has to be something we're not getting here," Lucas said, looking at the rules again.

Sarah sighed and slumped back down on the sofa. She'd pretty much given up.

As it neared the hour of twenty-three on the clock, Lucas and Sarah prepared for the worst.

"When he comes for one of us, let me do the talking," Sarah said sternly.

"Why, what are you planning?" Lucas asked in a worried tone.

"I'm going to try and take him by surprise," Sarah said nervously. "Come and help me as soon as you can."

"Even if we kill him, what are we going to do tomorrow?" Lucas said depressed. "And the day after that?"

"Don't think about it for now," Sarah said, gently caressing his face. "All we've got to think about for the moment is surviving tonight, okay?"

"I don't want to kill the Wreck – I mean Philip – tomorrow," he said sadly. "And I don't want either of us to... you know."

"And we won't," Sarah said defiantly. "If we can't solve this by tomorrow night then we'll all just have to die."

"Maybe Philip will tell us. He seems to be getting better every day," Lucas pondered.

"Like I said, don't worry about it until tomorrow," Sarah reaffirmed her point. "If we don't take Mitchell out of the picture then it won't matter."

Lucas nodded, and together they waited in agonising silence as the music finally stopped.

Mitchell didn't waste any time, and he arrived in the living room only minutes later wielding the sledgehammer in both hands. "I hope one of you is going to make this easy for me," he said evilly.

Sarah stepped forward, reaching for a knife she'd put in the back of her trousers. "Yes, I've decided–" she began.

Before she could even finish her sentence, the music had started to play again. Everyone's eyes went wide as they wondered what had happened.

"No." Mitchell stammered. "No, you couldn't have..."

He raced upstairs, and Lucas and Sarah followed at a safe distance. The stairs to the attic were down again and Mitchell was already halfway into the hatch when they caught up to him. They all gathered in the gloom and looked around bewildered.

There was another noose swinging where Komo had died, a few stacked up crates, and a fallen chair, but no Philip. Mitchell began searching everywhere in the dusty attic. He even looked under the blanket that was over Komo's corpse, until he finally noticed Philip's clothes in a scattered heap underneath the noose. Sarah and Lucas joined the brutish man next to the discarded clothing.

"If the music is on, does that mean he killed himself?" Sarah asked, puzzled.

"It looks like it, but where is his body?" Lucas asked.

Mitchell looked on sadly but didn't say a word.

"Maybe he tried it here but died somewhere else in the house?" Sarah said.

"I'll go check," Mitchell grumbled.

"Wait!" Lucas said, kneeling to the floor. He pulled a few torn pieces of paper from underneath the clothes and recognised Philip's scrawls. "He left a note."

"What's it say?" Mitchell demanded.

Lucas read the note out loud. "Dear Mitchell, Sarah, and Lucas. I'm sorry that I haven't been of much use until now, and thank you kindly for looking out for me for all this time. I've been trying to work things out and finally powered through the amnesia. I've learnt how to escape, with the house's help, but I'm afraid that I cannot tell you. To do so would rob you of your chance to be free of this place once and for all. What I can tell you is this; redemption is the key to escape. Remember what you are afraid to remember, embrace it, and beg forgiveness for what you've done. Only then will you truly be free. I hope with all my heart that you all find peace. Philip Doyle."

"He got out?" Sarah gasped.

"By killing himself," Mitchell grumbled.

"But Jacob and Leo killed themselves, and they didn't *disappear*," Sarah said. She was so tremendously confused that it was starting to make her head spin.

"Maybe because they weren't sorry," Lucas said, thinking on what he'd just read.

Both Sarah and Mitchell looked at him strangely as if he had spoken in a foreign language. Sarah couldn't speak for Mitchell, but forgiveness was the last thing that was on her mind.

DAY 10

The three survivors spent the rest of the night combing through the house, just to make sure that Philip the Wreck hadn't wound up somewhere else. They all came up empty handed. Somehow, the strange man had pulled his broken mind back together again and worked out what they were unable to; he had found a way out of the paranormal prison that was soon to be their grave, unless they too discovered it.

It took Sarah a ridiculously long time to fall asleep. Many times during the night she thought about crossing the room to snuggle up to Lucas, but she couldn't bring herself to cross that line. She was saddened that they hadn't met under different circumstances.

Although it felt like she had been awake the whole night, sleep did eventually hit her. The peaceful spell she'd been blessed with after the death of Jessica was definitely over, as once again her unconscious mind was filled with horrendous nightmares.

In her dreams she was sitting in her house again, all alone, shutting out the world beyond. She would get up for work and that would fly by, a blur of fake smiles and idle conversation. But she would always return to her empty house and sit alone, staring into space, suppressing the urge to scream and shout and tear the whole place apart. The days went by and still she sat there, ignoring calls, letting the mail pile up, and eventually she even stopped going to work.

Somewhere in the haze of depression a wordless voice began whispering into her ear, filling her head with unpleasant ideas and violent revenge fantasies. She didn't fight it as it grew louder and started pushing the person she once knew herself as out of existence. As the weeks turned into months and the months turned into years, Sarah was reborn anew, and every time she looked in the mirror she barely recognised the person looking back at her. She knew what she had to do.

Sarah woke up with a terrible migraine. The dream had felt like a lifetime and she was more exhausted than before she drifted off. She did her best to shake off the weird dream but it lingered at the back of her mind for the whole day, coupled with what Philip had written in his suicide note. Her mind was a battle between two sides, one that wanted to remember and one that didn't. The part of her that didn't want to know soon emerged victorious. Whatever animosity she felt towards her family was justified. She didn't need to remember the nitty-gritty details, she really didn't want to remember, and she certainly didn't want to feel *sorry* about whatever had happened to them.

The day was almost an exact repeat of the day before. Mitchell stayed out of Sarah and Lucas' way and they did the same to him. The only real difference was Lucas' spirits. After what had happened to Philip, he had regained some of the positive attitude that he'd had at the beginning of their ordeal in the House of Twelve. Sarah lost count of the times he'd read the letter and the house rules, and he began to annoy her about what she could remember of her life and her dreams. She made it quite clear that she didn't want to talk about it and that their biggest concern should be Mitchell's wrath, but that didn't stop him from going over his own clouded details.

"Sometimes it's my Dad that's going down the stairs," Lucas repeated, "and sometimes it's me. I hate to say it, but I think I pushed him."

"I don't think you did," Sarah said, bored. "You're too nice."

Lucas strained his mind, pressing his temples as he forced the memories out of the painful haze. "I think I was short on money, and he was old, old and on the way out. But then he started to get better..."

"So you pushed him and cashed in the inheritance early," Sarah said casually.

"How can you be so calm about that?" Lucas asked, shocked.

Sarah shrugged but then thought twice about her attitude. "I'm sorry, this fucking house has pushed me to the edge. I don't think anything would surprise me at this point."

"It's okay," Lucas said, trying to sound fine.

Sarah smiled, but there was something about the way he was looking at her that made her uneasy.

They weren't hungry, but they went to the kitchen for some food in the early evening anyway. Now that there were three people left, there was plenty of food and drink to go around, not that it seemed to matter to them anymore. Sarah began drinking some of the remaining spirits straight from the bottle, and Lucas gave her a disapproving look.

Sarah shrugged and sighed. "It's not like there isn't enough water to go around anymore. If we're coming to the end of... whatever this is, we might as well be a little bit merry." She handed the bottle to Lucas.

"Yeah," he reluctantly agreed, "I suppose you're right there." He took a big swig and it went down a lot better than he thought it would.

The iron door in the kitchen that Komo had previously unlocked (only to be presented with a bricked-up doorway) swung open, emitting a long screeching whine as it did. Pasted all over the bricks were scraps of newspaper articles, pictures, police reports, and other pieces of information about the unfortunate captives in the House of Twelve. Some of the writing had been obscured by thick black marker pen, and some of the pictures had been cut or had whole sections missing.

"What now?" Sarah moaned.

Lucas was quick to investigate. He scanned over the scrapbook-style display and quickly noticed a pattern. "Everyone is on here except for me, you, and Mitchell. They were all killers, criminals, or just very, *very* bad people. I suppose we are, too."

"Unless the house is messing with us again," Sarah said, *bored* of repeating what she felt was the obvious.

Ignoring Sarah's lack of interest, Lucas began reading out the bits of information he could put together as best he could, considering that a lot of the useful details had been blacked out or cut away.

According to the wall, Carl had in fact been a child sex offender, and the house's initial report was backed up by some newspaper articles. Dan the alcoholic had been driving under the influence and crashed into a tree, and his wife who was in the passenger's seat had died on impact. Melanie had drowned her children in the bathtub, but Lucas couldn't figure out why from the information at hand. Jacob had gone on a poisoning spree at his university in some kind of sociopathic revenge trip. Lucky Leo had become quite unlucky with his gambling habits and had turned to violent muggings to help fend off his loan sharks. Philip the Wreck was wanted by the police for several counts of fraudulent activity involving the vulnerable and the elderly. Jack was a rapist and murderer of young women, and on the other side of the coin, Jessica was a serial killer of men after her friend had been killed in a violent and abusive relationship. Lastly, Komo had indeed shot a bank security guard after what would have been her most successful heist to date went sour. Her accomplices were still on the run.

"I guess we're here to make amends," Lucas said thoughtfully.

"It's more likely that we're here to just suffer and die," Sarah said dryly.

"Think about it," Lucas said enthusiastically. "That's how Philip got out; he was genuinely sorry and took his own life for it."

Sarah didn't like the idea of taking her own life but she definitely didn't want to kill Lucas, which left her little choice. "I suppose after Mitchell is out of the way we've got no other option."

"So we've got to remember what it is we've done, properly remember, no matter how much it hurts us," Lucas said confidently.

"Let's try and survive tonight and work on that tomorrow," Sarah said, trying to push the conversation away from the remembering subject.

"Maybe we can convince Mitchell," Lucas said optimistically.

"Now you are talking out of your arse," Sarah said with a forced smile. "When he comes for us again let me do the talking, just like yesterday, and I'll take him by surprise... hopefully."

Lucas looked worried. "What if it goes wrong?"

"Then I suppose you'll have Mitchell for company tomorrow," she joked, but Lucas didn't seem amused by the notion at all.

It reached eleven at night quicker than either Sarah or Lucas expected. They had lost themselves in idle chatter about their hobbies and interests, and anything else to distract themselves from the paranormal prison they were sealed in or what they would have to do in order to escape it, not to mention the inevitable encounter with Mitchell that night.

Just like clockwork, Mitchell arrived for them as soon as the music stopped, once again wielding the sledgehammer like it was his own private weapon.

"I hope you've decided which one of you is next," Mitchell grumbled. His eyes were bloodshot and there were dark bags under them where he hadn't slept at all.

"I drew the short straw," Sarah lied, slowly approaching him like the night before. "Just make it quick."

"Wait," Lucas said. "Mitchell, we think we've worked out another way."

"There is no other way," Mitchell growled. "Only one of us will survive this and you know it's going to be me."

"But think about what happened to the Wreck!" Lucas shouted pleadingly. "He begged forgiveness and took his life for what he did—"

"Then he was a fool!" Mitchell spat back savagely. "They screwed me over, so I screwed them over back," he mumbled insanely, foaming at the mouth like a rabid dog. "They had no right taking my brother, no fucking right at all involving him!"

"Calm down," Lucas said, slowly moving forward. "We can talk this through..."

"*Get back*," Sarah hissed out of the side of her mouth to Lucas.

"I'm not sorry!" Mitchell roared. "I'm not sorry! I'll never be fucking sorry!"

Sarah quickly reached for the knife she had hidden down the back of her trousers and went to lunge at Mitchell's neck, but he batted her in the face with the handle of the hammer and sent her falling to the floor with a bloody nose. While Lucas was fumbling for his concealed knife, Mitchell raised the hammer above his head ready to bring it down on the wounded woman, but she deftly pulled out another small knife that had been tucked into her sock and stabbed it into the hulking man's leg. He screamed in agony and struggled to keep his grip on the sledgehammer, but he quickly recovered in a surge of pure bloodlust. Sarah scrambled away and only just escaped a heavy blow from the brutal hammer, when seemingly out of nowhere, Lucas leapt at Mitchell with his blade drawn. Mitchell was too preoccupied with his pursuit of Sarah to notice in time, and the knife slid into the brute's neck. Lucas' impromptu attack knocked Mitchell off his feet, and the beast of a man slammed into the floor with a massive thud. Lucas stabbed at him like a man possessed, and it was only until Sarah carefully stopped him that he seemed to register what he had done. Dropping the knife into the spreading pool of Mitchell's blood, Lucas embraced Sarah and shivered with self-induced fright. Sarah smiled slyly as she wiped her bloody nose and squeezed Lucas tightly.

DAY 11

Lucas had gone to sleep as soon as he had washed himself clean of Mitchell's blood. Sarah had thanked him graciously and had settled him in the blue bed, kissing him on the forehead before going to bed herself. It was just the two of them now, and together they would escape or die. She had to put the pillows over her head to muffle the awful cheesy music playing on repeat. She was sure that it was just her imagination, but it was so loud and hard to shut out.

Her dreams were chaotic and maddening. One moment she would be fighting for her life in a house full of strangers, far less diplomatic than the ones she had encountered in the House of Twelve. The next moment she would be burning in a sea of boiling blood, fighting to the death with her family, or something else barbaric and agonising. The strange encounters went on and on, always different but still following a similar pattern, until they became a blur of flashing scenarios flickering through her mind like a strobe light. Amid the mind-wrenching chaos, Sarah began to remember. She began to see herself as she truly was, and just as she was about to accept it, she shut it all out. Once again, she was all alone in total darkness. It was cold, lonely, and empty, but she preferred it there in the void compared to facing the truth. That was why she wasn't allowed to stay.

When Sarah got up, Lucas was already gone from the children's bedroom (apparently he hadn't been that settled after all), so she headed to the bathroom to wash before starting her last day in the House of Twelve.

She flinched when she saw that her reflection was acting completely independently. Sarah watched on horrified as a different version of herself, dressed in a little tight white dress, started applying bright red lipstick. The reflection seemed to notice Sarah staring and gave her a playful wink.

"Fuck you and fuck this stupid house," Sarah groaned angrily. Her patience for the strange prison and its tricks had long expired.

The reflection shrugged and started scrawling on its side of the mirror with the lipstick, writing backwards for Sarah's benefit, and eventually it spelled out 'you know what to do'. The reflection moved her body to the side and pointed to her backside. Sarah looked on, extremely confused until she realised that there was a knife tucked into her reflection's dress just above the waist. Sarah reached behind herself and felt that there was a small knife tucked into the waistline of her own trousers. The reflection smiled and disappeared, leaving only the words on the glass, and Sarah took her hand off the knife handle quickly. She was sure that she'd removed it the night before, and she definitely couldn't remember putting it back there after Mitchell's death.

Sarah left the bathroom in a hurry and went downstairs to find Lucas. He was playing detective at the bricked-up kitchen doorway again.

"There's more!" he said, partly eager and partly anxious.

"More articles and info?" Sarah asked half-heartedly while she ate some unbuttered bread.

"Yeah, Mitchell's story is up there now but there's nothing we didn't already know from last night. Most of the pen marks have disappeared and the pictures are complete." He hesitated and took a deep breath. "My story is up there, too."

Sarah walked over and stood beside him. Lucas pointed at a newspaper clipping that confirmed his back story, and Sarah chuckled. "That's not possible. Tell me you don't believe it?"

"Why shouldn't I?" Lucas said flatly. "After everything we've seen happen in here, you think it isn't a possibility?"

Sarah shook her head and read the gist of the report aloud in a mocking tone. "Double death in the Adams' house. Less than a week after self-made millionaire Trevor Adams fell to his death down a flight of stairs in his mansion, his son Lucas followed suit by falling down the same stairs only days after inheriting his father's properties and wealth. After a brief investigation the police have found no evidence to suggest that either death was suspicious, despite their coincidental nature. The Adams fortune is being left to charity, in accordance with Lucas' last Will and Testament."

Lucas looked at Sarah solemnly. "I changed my will after the guilt started to get to me. I thought it might make me feel better, knowing that after I was gone the leftover money would do some good. When it didn't take away that god-awful feeling, I started hitting the bottle. I never was that coordinated when I was drunk, and I remember trying to reach for the railings as I tumbled down those hardwood stairs."

"That would mean that you're dead, though," Sarah smirked.

"We're all dead, we're all dead," Lucas said, imitating Philip the Wreck's early ramblings.

Sarah sighed. "I can't deny the paranormal fucked-up weird stuff going on here, but I think that's a step too far. You know the house likes to play with us."

"Look, though," Lucas said pointing at the now complete stories on the wall. "The guard shot Komo right before he died, Carl was murdered by a grieving parent, here's a picture of Dan dead in the car beside his wife, Jacob poisoned himself when the police came for him..."

"All of that stuff can be fabricated," Sarah said in a frustrated tone.

"Everyone is on here except for you," Lucas said suspiciously. "I think it's because you're still in denial about your past."

Sarah laughed. "That's rich coming from the man who thinks that we're zombies or ghosts –"

"Or in some kind of *hell*," Lucas interrupted abruptly.

A shiver ran down Sarah's spine and a chill swept across her skin. She feared that Lucas was right, and it certainly would explain so much. She chided herself for the thought. She never put much stock in anything religious, and it just couldn't be possible. Sarah realised that she still expected her ordeal in the House of Twelve to end as quickly as it began, still expected to suddenly be somewhere else rubbing her eyes and discovering that it was all a bad dream. Maybe it would just take her death to wake up and achieve that sweet release.

"You need to remember for this to work," Lucas reminded her, snapping Sarah out of her deep contemplation.

"Yeah, and to seek forgiveness," Sarah said, trying to sound eager. "I'll work on it today," she lied. She would kill herself to be free, but she would never spend an ounce of forgiveness on her family, regardless of whatever wrongs she had committed against them.

For the rest of the day Sarah pretended to be meditating on some deep 'inner revelation', while Lucas tinkered about in the basement mixing what he hoped would be a quick and painless end to their incarceration in the House of Twelve. When Lucas would ask Sarah how she was doing, she would lie, fabricate some stories of her past, and then she would spend the rest of the conversation trying to change the subject. She liked Lucas, undeniably so, but he was grating on her so much that she was almost looking forward to the evening. She still wasn't ready to accept the fact that dying in the House of Twelve would actually mean her true death.

When the music stopped at the hour of twenty-three, Sarah and Lucas made a start on what was left of the alcohol in the kitchen. They were shaking out of nervousness at what awaited them both, and they hoped the booze would give them the courage to see it through.

"So you've definitely remembered?" Lucas asked for the hundredth time.

"For the last time, yes," Sarah droned, "and I'm very *sorry* for what I've done."

"Good... that's good," Lucas said, seemingly oblivious to Sarah's lack of forgiveness. "If only we'd figured this out sooner, we could have saved the others," he added remorsefully.

"Maybe they'll get their chance yet," Sarah mumbled, remembering her dreams of the other houses, and then she quickly shunned the thought and all the horrifying realisations that came with it.

"Let's hope so," Lucas said honestly.

Sarah didn't know whether she admired or despised his righteousness. Her head felt like it was splitting in half again.

"You ready?" he asked when she didn't answer.

"Yeah," Sarah replied slowly. "Will it hurt?"

"Maybe for a little bit," Lucas replied unconfidently. "But it should be over quick. There's some potent stuff down in the basement and I've mixed the worst of the worst."

Sarah leaned in and kissed him gently. She didn't know quite where it came from, but acted purely on instinct. "Good luck," she whispered.

"You too, Sarah," he said in return, and gave her a longer, more intimate kiss before passing her a tall glass of noxious eye-watering chemicals.

In unison, they both held their breaths and raised the glasses to their lips. Sarah looked fearfully into Lucas' green eyes and he looked back into hers. They began to tip the glasses and the liquid trickled close to their mouths, and then for a split second, Lucas hesitated. Sarah finally snapped.

The accumulation of Sarah's repressed memories, dreadful dreams, and distressing ordeals in the House of Twelve sparked like a flame and ignited like wildfire across her turbulent mind. She smashed the glass of chemicals into the side of Lucas' head. His expression of surprise and betrayal was marred by stinging toxins and cut with splinters of glass.

Sarah leapt on him and drew the knife she'd kept in the back of her trousers. It seemed so obvious to her now why she'd put it back in there, just like her reflection had reminded her.

"It's you!" she screamed. "You tricked me! This has all been because of you!" Again, the fact that Lucas had locked them all in the house to suffer for his amusement was so clear to her.

She stabbed him over and over, and every time the knife pierced his flesh and slid free again a flash of memory sparked into the darkness in her mind and illuminated the void with images. Sarah remembered the years of depression following her sister Lisa's affair with Darren, and the unbearable humiliation of finding out on her wedding day never ever faded. She remembered her failed suicide attempt after finding out Lisa was to marry Darren, she remembered being shunned by her family as an 'attention seeker', and she remembered wishing that Lisa and Darren's twin daughters would die in childbirth. Finally, she remembered dolling herself up, taking a fine selection of knives and tools, and visiting her family. She started with her parents, and after a long and dangerously fast drive she moved on to the twin girls, who had just turned six that week. Lisa and Darren had been woken by the screams, and Darren had hit Sarah hard in the head with a bat, but she'd played dead and stabbed him in the back while he was grieving the loss of his daughters. Sarah still remembered the feeling of gratitude after seeing that there was still enough life in his eyes to witness her slitting Lisa's throat in front of him. Afterwards, she had doused the house in petrol and set it aflame, just as she had done with her parents' house. Sarah remembered how urgently she had left the property in her sports car, her sick desire for revenge still not sated, and the momentary flash of fear when the police car came out of nowhere...

Lucas was long dead. His blood was all over the kitchen and Sarah was soaked by the time her arms grew too tired to continue. She screamed at the top of her lungs and muffled the background music that was playing once again. With her madness subsiding, the realisation of what she'd done truly dawned on her. There was no chance that Lucas was responsible for her being in the House of Twelve, and despite his brief pause with the glass of poison, there was no way of knowing whether he would have taken his life or not. The more Sarah thought about it, the more she wondered if she'd even seen the hesitation or not. Then something whispered to her from the back of her mind, a wordless voice that filled her head with a sense of power and superiority, and in accepting her lunacy she realised why she had lied to herself. Sarah had tricked herself into killing Lucas so that she would survive the House of Twelve.

"There, they're all dead!" Sarah yelled at the ceiling. "I win, I'm the last one standing, and I hope you're fucking happy – now *let me out!*"

She stood in the blood-soaked kitchen, staring at the ceiling with her glazed eyes as if the house owed her a response for her 'victory', and to her relief she heard the letterbox clattering faintly from the hallway. Sarah rushed in and saw that there was a letter addressed to her.

"Finally," Sarah muttered to herself. "You'd better be telling me how to get out," she said, speaking to the envelope.

She unfolded the paper with her bloody, shaking hands and read the words aloud. "Dear Miss Sarah Fischer. We apologise, but it seems as though there has been some confusion regarding your stay in the House of Twelve. If you consult the house rules, you will see that it is in no way implied that being the last survivor will guarantee your escape. In fact, it reaffirms the principle that redemption is the only way you will ever be free. Don't give up hope. You still have one more day, not to mention all of your memories, to make things right once and for all. Kindest regards, the House of Twelve."

Sarah tore up the letter and broke down into hysterical tears.

DAY 12

Sarah didn't sleep that night. Instead she cried hysterically by the doorway, absorbed in the sheer hopelessness of her situation. Her mind raced between feelings of anger, guilt, fear, shame, and hate-filled rage. She had killed Lucas for nothing and there was no way back. Now she was all alone with no way out, and the medley of pain and emotions in her head was overwhelming. Finally in the early hours of the morning, in a moment of maddening defiance, she stormed into the front room, stepped over Mitchell's blanket-covered body, and picked up the sledgehammer.

"You want to play games?" she screamed at the walls. "How do you like this one?"

Sarah smashed the living room to pieces, not even pausing to wait for the lights to come back on after they would cut out, and quickly carried her rampage on to the other rooms. The music began growing louder, to the point where it hurt her ears, but still she carried on her quest for carnage persistently. Sarah wasn't sure what she was trying to achieve. She hoped that somehow she was hurting the house, but the violence and destruction filled her with a sense of satisfaction either way. It reminded her of when she had torn her own house to pieces, right before the killings.

She ignored the scrapbook-style clippings on the brickwork in the kitchen and tore them to shreds, even the new ones showing pictures of her crashed sports car. Sarah was convinced that the House of Twelve was trying to fuck with her, and she wasn't going to have it anymore. She did her best not to look at Lucas' lifeless corpse and forced herself to forget that it was there.

Her sister's daughters were in the bathroom mirror crying and wailing, just like they had done before she had stabbed the life out of them. "You want me to be sorry?" she screamed at the bathroom mirror, which was now displaying a black nothingness as if it was carved from obsidian. "I'll never be sorry for those fuckers! Never! They ruined my life!" Sarah smashed the mirror into pieces and trashed the bathroom before moving on to the bedrooms.

She was beginning to tire but carried on relentlessly. The lights were beginning to switch off for longer before flickering back on, but she continued her vandalism in the darkness. The music died down to its normal droning volume and allowed Sarah to regain her hearing. Her arms ached so badly that after she was satisfied with her destruction of the children's bedroom and the lights had switched off to punish or discourage her, she waited and caught her breath until they came back on again. When they did, she saw that the house had finally responded, but definitely not in a way that she wanted.

The wallpaper and paint from the walls in the House of Twelve had been removed, leaving only a plain dirty grey surface in every room, and covering them were scribbles and scrawls written presumably by other captives. There must have been thousands of messages, written by people in varying stages of psychological breakdowns, all over the house.

Sarah let go of the hammer and traced her finger along some of the desperate messages. "Help, let me out, nothing but darkness outside, kill at twenty-three live at twenty-four, twelve, twelve, twelve," she read aloud. "We're all dead, we're all dead," which she recognised as Philip the Wreck's writing. "How is that possible when he just died?" she asked herself.

"You already know," the background music whispered from behind her. "Your *friend* figured it out."

Sarah turned around so fast that it hurt her neck, but there was no one behind her. Her heart was pumping so hard that she thought it might burst from her chest, and then she saw that the sledgehammer had disappeared. The house had replaced it with a pencil.

More flashes of memories stormed into her mind. She thought she had remembered everything, but new images appeared nonetheless. Sarah was standing at the exposed walls but in a different house, adding more messages and doodles to the rest whilst giggling like a lunatic. Then she was doing the same again in a different house but this time she was crying, and another time she was bleeding from a severe chest wound. There were literally dozens of memories of reaching the very same point.

"It's just not possible," she muttered.

Then she remembered writing something in a very similar house, above the fireplace just over the creepy clock. Sarah grabbed the pencil off the floor and ran down to the living room. It, too, was covered in desperate and almost nonsensical scrawls, but there was one message amongst the others that stood out. Just like she had remembered, there was a message on the wall right above the clock.

"Redemption is the key to escape, be sorry and take your life to escape. Fuck, fuck, fuck! It's easier said than done!" Sarah read her own words and then copied them a few inches above just to confirm that it was in fact her own writing.

"Fine," she sighed in defeat. "You want me to kill myself? You've got it – I won't give you the satisfaction of gassing me!" she yelled defiantly.

"We want you to be sorry..." the voice within the music whispered.

"I'm sorry," Sarah said unconvincingly through gritted teeth. "There, all done! Happy?"

No response came, but instead the clock's single hour hand zoomed around to the hour of twenty-three and stopped there as the music switched off. For a moment Sarah hoped that it had broken, but after staring at the hand for a minute she sighed with disappointment as it moved along slightly towards twenty-four.

"You want to play it like that? Fine, then we'll play dirty!" Sarah shouted.

Sarah stomped down to the basement and began carting up any liquid she could see with a flammable sign on it. She started to douse the house in all manner of eye-watering chemicals. Her earlier rampage had given her an almost inexhaustible supply of kindling for what she was planning next, and she carried on until each room's walls, floors, shattered furnishings, and any dead bodies were damp with volatile liquids. It was just like when she had done the same to Lisa and Darren's house, and to her parents' house.

"You want me to kill myself?" Sarah asked the house angrily. "Well, then you're coming with me."

Sarah sniggered as she found a lighter in one of the kitchen drawers. The house smelled so bad and the chemicals were giving her a pounding headache, but it wouldn't matter for much longer.

"Goodbye, thanks for having me," she snarled sarcastically before going to move her thumb downwards on the lighter to end it all.

Her confident smile quickly faded. She couldn't do it. It wasn't that the lighter wouldn't work, or that her hand wouldn't respond, but she just couldn't bring herself to die.

"Come on, Sarah, come on," she said, prepping herself for the big moment; but still, nothing.

"On the count of three," Sarah said confidently, breathing in and out heavily. "One... two... three..." After a long pause and with an angry hiss, she threw the lighter on the floor and stamped on it. She just couldn't do it.

Sarah fell to the damp stinking floor and wept, and when she looked over at Lucas' bloodied body, she realised that it hadn't been him that had hesitated the night before. It had been her. She cried uncontrollably, feeling nauseated from the sickening stench of the chemicals, until the clock ticked over to twenty-four and the gas filled the house. Her eyes, mouth, and nose stung severely as the gas engulfed her, and her lungs felt as though they had been pumped full of fire as she began to black out. Her last sensation was that of pure and total agony.

EPILOGUE

S trange images of her family flashed through her mind amongst violent red flashes, and were interrupted only by eerie still pictures of household interiors. Bricked up windows, sealed doors and overwhelming visions of endless darkness flowed into her turbulent dream. Along with them came pleasant yet creepy music, like the type that played in elevators and telephone on-hold tracks, and it droned through her skull relentlessly. As irritating as it was, for some strange reason she feared more than anything that it would end.

Sarah awoke in what appeared to be a modern house living room. The walls were clean and white, the floor was polished wooden panelling, fancy modern art hung from the walls, and the furnishings looked like they had come straight out of a designer catalogue. However, a very strange clock sat upon one of the room's shelves and looked extremely out of place. Sarah's tired mind began to warm up and she realised that she couldn't remember much about herself or anything of her past, and she couldn't remember ever coming to the house that she was in. An annoying tune was playing faintly in the background, not very loud but definitely not quiet enough to ignore, and it was the exact same tune from her strange dream. In a surge of panic, she realised that the windows were bricked-up and that there were people she had never seen before lying unconscious on the furniture and floor. Quickly and quietly, Sarah got up and looked for the way out, but when she found the hallway her path was blocked by a sturdy metal door. It would not budge, despite how hard she tried to move it.

"No way out that way, only black, redemption is the only way..." a shabby 'wreck' of a man mumbled from the opposite corner of the hallway.

Sarah jumped out of fright and surprise and backed towards the door, but when she looked at the unshaven, dirty man, something stirred in her memory. His scruffy auburn hair and scared green eyes sparked some sort of recognition. Did she know him? The name 'Liam', no, *Luke* sprang to mind, but she couldn't quite put her finger on what it was. Or maybe he was 'Adam'? It was no use; she couldn't think of it. He did look as though he would be rather handsome if he was cleaned up, and so she tried to force herself to remember him, but it made her head hurt and filled her with an awful sense of guilt, shame, and regret, so she stopped.

"I'm sorry, Dad, I'm sorry," the auburn-haired 'wreck' whimpered, as Sarah realised that the other people in the house were starting to wake up.

She carefully made her way back into the living room, staying on guard in case one of the others was dangerous, and saw that one of them was holding what looked like a black leather-bound menu. It was titled in gold lettering with 'The House Rules'.

ALSO BY THIS AUTHOR

The Book Wielder Saga: Dreamleaf Blues

Excerpt Below:

Her veins felt as though they had been set aflame, and Genevieve tried to roar out in pain but no sound escaped her mouth. She couldn't breathe and she couldn't move. Genie knew that she was dying and she wished for it to be over, but the suffering simply wouldn't end. The relentless anguish grew so bad that all other thoughts vanished completely and were replaced with a deafening cacophony of agony.

She stirred from her slumber and wondered if the unbearable torment had all been a dream, but when Genevieve opened her eyes she couldn't see properly. Genie tried to reach for her face but her arms were stuck in place, and she tried to move her legs but they too were restrained.

Genevieve's mind snapped into focus, and she realised that her nose and mouth were covered with something uncomfortably tight. She couldn't breathe in the slightest.

In a panic, Genie tugged at her restraints with all her might. Her body ached all over and the effort was incredibly painful, but nothing as bad as the horrible sensation that had preceded her awakening. She heard tearing and feared that it was her own muscles, but with a sudden sharp snap and the sound of cracking wood, Genevieve sat upright.

She fumbled at her mouth and felt thick strips of duct tape encasing the lower half of her face, and paper was flapping over her eyes. Scratching, scraping, and peeling frantically, she ripped every last strip from her face. Genevieve yelped as the duct tape tore away from her mouth and she was sure that she'd lost some skin. She took in deep panicked breaths and was surprised that she felt no better than when she was gagged.

Genevieve turned her attention to the top half of her face, and could feel some thick paper had been taped to her forehead. She carefully peeled it away to avoid losing any more skin.

When her eyes adjusted she was welcomed by the sight of her own bedroom, although her usually neat and tidy room looked like it had been hit by a tornado. The curtains were closed, and someone had slung thick blankets over the curtain rails to block the windows further. Barely any light crept inside her bedroom, but she could see everything as clear as day.

Genevieve let out a short sigh of relief, grateful to be in her home, although she still acknowledged the fact that she was in grave danger. She looked down at her arms which were deathly pale, and saw thick ropes had been woven around her wrists. Genevieve gasped when she realised that she'd snapped them with ease. Genie reached over and grabbed her leg restraints, for if someone came for her she wanted to be ready, and the strong rope tore under the lightest touch from her nails and was easily pulled to shreds in her firm grip.

"What the fuck is going on?" Genie whispered to herself, her voice raspy and dry. She desperately needed something to drink.

It was then Genevieve noticed that the paper which had been covering her face, which was an entire half of one of her notepads, had a message written on it in crude, brutish handwriting. With a crushing sense of dread, Genie read the note:

Good morning, Bitch –
If you're reading this then you survived, kind of. If not... whoopsie!
Either way, we'll be round to deal with you in a night or two.
Till then, don't go outside, don't call anyone (we'll know!) and keep those curtains shut!
If you stay put like a good little girl then we won't have to go visit your parents Don and Betty, and their good neighbours Martha and Julian, over in Legentium.
We might even help you find your friend...

Genevieve dropped the note and let it fall slowly towards the floor. She had no idea what was happening to her, and the people responsible were threatening her and Anna's family. However, the last bit of the message piqued her interest, and despite the nerve-wracking situation Genie was still determined to find the truth about Annabelle's fate.

She climbed off the bed, forcing her weary limbs into action, and approached her bedroom door. Genevieve placed her ear against the painted wood and listened for any activity on the other side. She waited there for at least ten minutes and heard absolutely nothing.

Not wanting to chance anything, Genevieve decided to peek out of the window. Although she didn't want to provoke the note's writers, Genie couldn't resist checking, and her room overlooked the front of the building. If anyone was keeping tabs on her then she might be able to see them, and just what she was up against.

Genevieve pulled the sheet and curtain aside a mere fraction of an inch at a time, and finally moved her head over enough to glance at the road below.

There was no one parked out front, and she couldn't see anyone suspicious on the green opposite or the deep thick forest beyond that. Genie's eyes were working remarkably well, and if she strained hard enough then distant objects came into focus with crystal clear clarity.

Children were playing ball games with their parents in the warm sun, and groups of older youths were hanging about, trying to look as cool and blasé as they possibly could to the opposite sex while they listened to Imperia's latest musical hits on their massive portable radios. If Genevieve tried really hard, she could faintly make out the music being played.

"It must be the weekend..." Genevieve whispered to herself. Somehow, she had lost most of the week.

The warm sun kissed Genie's face through her window pane, and she closed her eyes for a moment. The strong heat reminded Genevieve of her trip to Tropica, and she wanted to go back in time so badly, just to savour every second of those carefree days on her gap year with Annabelle. Everything had been so simple, and Genie wished it had stayed that way.

The heat from outside intensified, and Genie wondered why it was so hot. It looked like a normal day, and the people she could see were all wearing regular clothes. She looked upwards; there were barely any clouds in the sky but the sun was burning intently, and to Genevieve it felt as though someone had lit a magnesium flare next to her face. She quickly clenched her eyes shut and could hear her flesh cooking like sizzling barbequed meat. With a sharp squeal, Genie recoiled from the window.

She kept her eyes closed tightly and fumbled for the door. In a blind panic, she smashed through it as though it had been made of cheap MDF and skirted around the apartment until she found the bathroom. She felt for the sink and turned the handle as far as it would go. Genevieve dunked her face in the cool water until it was numb. She slowly opened her eyes and winced at the horrific sight of her own reflection. Her skin had burnt, blistered, and peeled down to the muscle tissue, and her irises were a striking shade of blood red. Genie stared at herself in shock, forgetting about the how and why, and her strangely imposed captivity, and tried to wrap her head around the fact that she was scarred for life. Even the best reconstructive surgery on the planet (which she couldn't even afford) wouldn't be able to fix her face. Then her eyes went wide with surprise.

"What the fuck...?" she breathed in awe. Her damaged face was slowly, but surely, regenerating.

Genevieve watched on mesmerised as the blisters receded and thin trickles of blood spread across her ruined face, leaving trails of repaired flesh in their wake. Her face was as good as new, and her complexion was even better than before, but her irises remained red. Genevieve also had two new protruding fangs beside her regular straight white teeth.

After gawping at her flattering reflection for a few minutes, the shock and surprise ebbed away, and Genevieve once again realised the gravity of the situation. Genie didn't know what she was, her throat was dry, her stomach ached with hunger, and she couldn't even guarantee that she was alone in the apartment.

Genie knew that making sure that she was secure, at least for the time being, should've been her top priority. However, the urge to quench her thirst was so great that she just couldn't resist. She turned the water back on and cupped the cold liquid with her hands, slurping it up ungracefully. Genevieve drank until her stomach was full and she felt physically sick, but her thirst remained unabated.

Groaning miserably, she turned her attention to the only matter she could solve. Even though she had blundered into the bathroom when her face had been scolded by the outside world, she assumed that the people responsible for her situation weren't above playing with their prey, from the way the note had been taped to her head. She looked at the partially open bathroom door fearfully, knowing that somebody could be lurking on the other side.

She quickly looked for a weapon but couldn't find anything substantial to wield. Genie took a deep breath, steadied her nerves, and carefully crept into the living room. She cringed as the bathroom door creaked open noisily, and Genevieve swiftly looked around at her living room for threats.

The rectangular room was a complete mess, just like her bedroom had been, and the shattered door added to the disorderedly look. Genevieve stared at the splintered wood in disbelief – it looked as though a rhino had stampeded through it – but she quickly snapped her focus away. There were more pressing matters at hand than whatever was happening to her body.

Her eyes darted around the dark, messy living room, rapidly checking for people hiding behind the overturned furniture, but she was alone. Genevieve picked up a long, sharp piece of broken wood, and preceded to the apartment's small kitchen. There was no one inside, and Genie discarded the wood and upgraded to a long kitchen knife instead.

Genevieve checked every cupboard, every wardrobe, and any hiding place she could think of. Satisfied that she was alone, Genie entered Annabelle's room. She grimaced when she saw the ruined room, as she had done her best to leave it just the way Annabelle had left it, only tidier. Like all the other rooms, its curtains had been reinforced with her spare sheets, and after the incident in her own room Genevieve was happy to leave them that way. All of Anna's money, Dreamleaf, and Tropican cannabis were missing. However, Genie still let out a sigh of relief when she found no sign of strangers within it.

As Genie tidied her friend's overly pink room, she mused about her own personal condition. Someone had smashed her face into the Woodsholme Grill's backroom door, but there was no sign of damage to her head. The sunlight had roasted her face through a window pane, and she had then watched as the damage repaired itself. Her eyes were crimson red, her senses were immensely better than they had been, and she was abnormally stronger than before. She had long fangs and was also unable to satisfy her thirst.

Genevieve finished placing Annabelle's furnishings back to where they belonged and made her friend's bed with loving care. She sat herself down on the soft pink sheets and studied her pale hands in a daze. Genie had read enough fantasy books to know what category of supernatural phenomena she belonged to.

"I'm a Vampire..." she whispered aloud, and felt incredibly stupid for doing so.

Conspiracy theories about Vampires, Werewolves, and spell-casting Mages had always been a part of Mydia's culture and had been woven into works of fiction since ancient times, but now Genevieve was living proof that they were in fact very real.

She ran her tongue along her smooth, viciously sharp fangs as she thought about her next move. Something – or someone – supernatural had taken an interest in her that night at the restaurant, and Genevieve was certain that she'd heard Big Dave and the other gang leaders being murdered. She assumed that those responsible were Vampires and had chosen to turn her on the side of their night-time killing spree. She remembered the liquid that had been poured down her throat and ignited her insides, and assumed it was blood. Genie couldn't help but chuckle at the fact she was self-diagnosing herself based on works of fiction. What she did know for sure was that the people who had turned and restrained her were extremely dangerous, and she would be a fool not to heed their threatening note. For the sake of hers and Annabelle's parents, she would stay put and meet her makers.

All she could do was wait. Genie cleaned the apartment from top to bottom, which helped to keep her mind off the insane turn of events and the ever-growing thirst and hunger. She raided the kitchen, and although the food tasted good, it did nothing to abate the pain in her stomach.

"Guess I need blood..." she scoffed both jokingly and fearfully.

Genie discarded her filthy waitress uniform which was caked in her own dried blood, and took a long hot bath. She closed her eyes and tried to relax, but her insides churned so much that she struggled to lay still. Genevieve dried herself off and dressed herself in a comfortable pair of black leggings and a long white t-shirt.

She missed the college's computers, with their text-based roleplaying games and the challenging turn-based strategy games. She tried to do some writing on one of her many notepads, but all she could manage was a dozen lines of 'I'm hungry' before giving up completely.

Genevieve did her best to keep her spirits high, but the sense of dread and fear of the frightening unknown, coupled with the incredible discomfort in her throat and stomach, quickly won the battle. She wished that the Dreamleaf hadn't been robbed, and resorted to necking down shots from a bottle of whiskey that had survived the pillaging of the apartment instead.

After a long miserable day, the sun set and the twin moons rose in its place. Genevieve had grown progressively drunker as time stretched on, and she found herself throwing nervous glances towards the front door. The urge to escape grew wilder as night fell, and she had to keep talking herself out of running away and never coming back.

"Mum and Dad, Martha and Julian, Annabelle..." Genie recited over and over like a prayer.

She staggered over to the long living room window and pulled down the random assortment of sheets covering it. She threw open the curtains and drank in the night. Genie looked out of her first-floor apartment and out at the moonstruck fields, trees, and buildings. She had never seen the evening with such clearness, but it was the people walking along the pavements that drew her interest. Genevieve could feel their warmth, their lifeblood coursing through their bodies, and the pumping of their beating hearts. She didn't just want their blood, she wanted to eat them whole, and Genevieve had to use all her restraint to stop herself from leaping through the window and tearing into their flesh. She threw the sheets back in place, ran into the bathroom and closed the door, just to put something between her and the delicious looking people below. When she caught her reflection out of the corner of her eye, Genevieve received another unpleasant surprise.

Her beautiful complexion had been replaced with patchy greying skin, she had dark bags under her eyes, and her new red eyes were violently bloodshot. Genevieve's veins were darkening and more of her teeth were growing into sharp points. Genie shied away and spent the night huddled in a ball beside her bathtub.

Genevieve was a wreck by the time that morning finally arrived. All her skin had turned grey, her mouth was filled with razor sharp fangs, and her fingernails had elongated into blade-like talons. Her face was looking better, but not in a human way. Her features were sharper and even further defined, her eyes were pure red slits that leaked seduction, the bags under her eyes had darkened further and it looked like she was wearing thick black make-up, and her hair was longer, fuller, and moved on its own accord in tantalising rhythmic waves.

Hunger became Genevieve's entire world that day, and every minute seemed like an hour. She paced around the apartment aimlessly, and switched between stalking like a hunched over beast and gliding along with elegant inhuman grace. Genie could hear her elderly next-door neighbours moving around, and she wanted to smash through the meagre wall to get to them.

The night came around again, and Genevieve didn't know how she'd held out for so long without losing her mind completely or murdering every person that she'd sensed passing by. She tried to stay focused on the parents and Annabelle, but truthfully, imagining people just made her hungrier. She was literally scratching at the dividing wall when the front door swung open...